the **wave**

THE EXCHANGE

**What happens
when loyalty is
unquestioned?**

the
wave

Todd Strasser

 HAMPTON-BROWN

The Wave by Todd Strasser
Copyright © 1981 by Random House, Inc., and T.A.T. Communications Company
Cover illustration by Jon C. Lund
Published by arrangement with Random House Children's Books
a division of Random House, Inc. New York, New York, U.S.A.
All rights reserved.

On-Page Coach™ (introductions, questions, on-page glossaries), The Exchange,
back cover summary © Hampton-Brown.

Hampton-Brown
P.O. Box 223220
Carmel, California 93922
800-333-3510
www.hampton-brown.com

Printed in the United States of America

ISBN-13: 978-0-7362-3185-5
ISBN-10: 0-7362-3185-4

08 09 10 11 12 13 14 15 10 9 8 7 6 5 4 3

FOREWORD

The Wave is based on a true incident that occurred in a high school history class in Palo Alto, California, in 1969. For three years afterward, according to the teacher, Ron Jones, no one talked about it. "It was," he said, "one of the most frightening events I have ever experienced in the classroom."

"The Wave" disrupted an entire school. The novel dramatizes the incident, showing how the powerful forces of group pressure that have pervaded many historic movements and cults can persuade people to join such movements and give up their individual rights in the process—sometimes causing great harm to others. The full impact on the students of what they lived through and learned is realistically portrayed in the book that follows.

In addition to the novel, *The Wave* has been made into a one-hour television show for ABC by Virginia L. Carter, an executive director at Tandem Productions and T.A.T. Communications Company.

HARRIET HARVEY COFFIN
Project Consultant
T.A.T. Communications Company

INTRODUCTION

Todd Strasser's novel *The Wave* is based on an experiment that took place in a high school classroom in California in 1969. It began when Ron Jones's history class was studying World War II and the mass killings carried out by Hitler's Nazi Germany. Jones's students questioned how German citizens at that time could claim they did not know about the murder of more than 6 million people. The students did not understand why more Germans had not tried to stop the Nazis. So Jones decided to create an experiment to teach his students a lesson about power.

In his experiment, Jones tried to create an environment similar to the one created by Hitler in Nazi Germany. He emphasized discipline, conformity, and loyalty. As students participated in the experiment, known as the Third Wave, their behavior quickly changed. Students practiced strict rules of discipline. They wore armbands to distinguish themselves from nonmembers. Members were full of hope and **idealism** . They believed the movement would help the

Key Concepts

idealism *n.* ideas of perfection

school. The movement did improve the school's **morale**. But soon, members began to harass the students who refused to join the Third Wave. Students who disagreed with their practices were threatened.

The experiment lasted only one week. Jones later described it as a "nightmare." Afterward, Jones's students did not want to talk about it. Jones never imagined his experiment would create so much **controversy**.

Throughout history, there have been cases of people blindly following leaders regardless of how wrong the leaders' practices may be. When this happens, scandals and abuses result. Some scholars and historians believe that these abuses are caused by a "fascist mentality." This mentality leads people to give up their rights as individuals and to conform to the group's ideas. People who support fascism believe that a code of strict discipline and loyalty to a strong leader promote social order. They believe that they are **superior** to people who do not follow this code. In *The Wave*, Ben Ross's students believe that devotion to the group can bring them better grades, a winning football team, and social equality among their classmates. What they do

Key Concepts

morale *n.* the well-being of a group

controversy *n.* public disagreement or debate

superior *adj.* higher in quality, rank, or status

not realize is that they are duplicating behavior that led to one of the darkest periods of the twentieth century, the Holocaust.

The Wave was well received by readers when it was published in 1981. Now, many schools in Germany have included the novel in their classes. The author, Todd Strasser, hopes that his book helps people realize how easy it can be for individuals to give up their **identity** and conform to a group. That way, horrible events like the Holocaust will never happen again.

What is Fascism?

During World War II, Italy and Germany had fascist governments. These are characteristics of a fascist government:

- strict governmental control over all aspects of life, including society, culture, and economy
- loyalty to a single leader
- the belief that a nation, state, or race is superior to others
- use of popular language that encourages extreme nationalism and promises to make the country a dominant power

Key Concepts

identity *n.* individuality; a person's uniqueness

CHAPTER 1

Laurie Saunders sat in the publications office at Gordon High School chewing on the end of a Bic pen. She was a pretty girl with short light-brown hair and **an almost perpetual** smile that only disappeared when she was upset or chewing on Bic pens. Lately she'd been chewing on a lot of pens. In fact, there wasn't a single pen or pencil in her pocketbook that wasn't worn down on the butt end from nervous **gnawing**. Still, **it beat** smoking.

Laurie looked around the small office, a room filled with desks, typewriters, and light tables. At that moment there should have been kids at each one of those typewriters, **punching out** stories for *The Gordon Grapevine*, the school paper. The art and layout staff should have been working at

....

an almost perpetual always had a
gnawing chewing
it beat it was better than
punching out writing, typing

the light tables, **laying out** the next issue. But instead the room was empty except for Laurie. The problem was that it was a beautiful day outside.

Laurie felt the plastic tube of the pen crack. Her mother had warned her once that someday she would chew on a pen until it splintered and a long plastic **shard would lodge** in her throat and she would choke to death on it. Only her mother could have come up with that, Laurie thought with a sigh.

She looked up at the clock on the wall. Only a few minutes were left in the period anyway. There was no rule that said anyone had to work in the publications office during **their free periods**, but they all knew that the next edition of *The Grapevine* was due out next week. Couldn't they give up their Frisbees and cigarettes and suntans for just a few days in order to get an issue of the paper out on time?

Laurie put her pen back in her pocketbook and started to gather up her notebooks for the next period. It was hopeless. For the three years she'd been on staff, *The Grapevine* had always been late. And now that she was the **editor-in-chief** it made no difference. The paper would be done when everyone got around to doing it.

....

laying out putting together; designing
shard would lodge piece of plastic would get stuck
their free periods the times they did not have class
editor-in-chief person in charge of the paper

Pulling the door of the publications office closed behind her, Laurie stepped out into the hall. It was practically empty now; the bell to change classes had not yet rung, and there were only a few students around. Laurie walked down a few doors, stopped outside a classroom, and peered through the window.

Inside, her best friend, Amy Smith, a petite girl with thick, curly, **Goldilocks** hair, was trying to endure the final moments of Mr. Gabondi's French class. Laurie had taken French with Mr. Gabondi the year before and it had been one of the most **excruciatingly** boring experiences of her life. Mr. Gabondi was a short, dark, heavyset man who always seemed to be sweating, even on the coldest winter days. When he taught, he spoke in a dull **monotone** that could easily put the **brightest** student to sleep, and even though the course he taught was not difficult, Laurie recalled how hard it had been to pay enough attention to get an *A*.

Now watching her friend struggle to stay interested, Laurie decided she needed some cheering up. So, positioning herself outside the door where Amy could see her but Gabondi could not, Laurie crossed her eyes and made an idiotic face. Amy reacted by putting her hand over her

....

Goldilocks blonde
excruciatingly painfully
monotone voice
brightest smartest

mouth to keep from laughing. Laurie made another face and Amy tried not to look, but she couldn't help turning back to see what her friend was doing next. Then Laurie **did her famous fish face**: she pushed her ears out, crossed her eyes, and puckered her lips. Amy was trying so hard not to laugh that tears started to roll down her cheeks.

Laurie knew she shouldn't make any more faces. Watching Amy was too funny—anything could make her laugh. If Laurie did any more, Amy would probably fall out of her seat and roll into the aisle between the desks. But Laurie couldn't resist. Turning her back to the door to create some suspense, she screwed up her mouth and eyes, and then spun around.

Standing at the door was a very angry Mr. Gabondi. Behind him Amy and the rest of her class were **in hysterics**. Laurie's jaw dropped. But before Gabondi could **reprimand** her, the bell rang and his class was suddenly spilling out into the hall around him. Amy came out holding her sides in pain from laughing so hard. As Mr. Gabondi glared at them, the two girls went off arm in arm toward their next class, too out of breath to laugh anymore.

....

did her famous fish face made a face that looked like a fish
in hysterics laughing a lot
reprimand yell at

In the classroom where he taught history, Ben Ross crouched over a film projector, trying to **thread a film** through the complex maze of rollers and lenses. This was his fourth attempt and he still hadn't gotten it right. Frustrated, Ben ran his fingers through his wavy brown hair. All his life he had been **befuddled** by machinery—film projectors, cars, even the self-service pump at the local gas station **drove him bananas**.

He had never been able to figure out why he was so inept in that way, and so when it came to anything mechanical, he left it to Christy, his wife. She taught music and choir at Gordon High, and at home she was in charge of anything that **required manual dexterity**. She often joked that Ben couldn't even be trusted to change a light bulb correctly, although Ben insisted this was an exaggeration. He had changed a number of light bulbs in his life and could only recall breaking two in the process.

Thus far in his career at Gordon High—Ben and Christy had been teaching there for two years—he had managed to hide his mechanical inabilities. Or rather, they had been overshadowed by his growing reputation as an outstanding young teacher. Ben's students spoke of his intensity—the

....

thread a film slide the movie strip
befuddled confused
drove him bananas made him crazy; confused him
required manual dexterity needed to be fixed

way he got so interested and involved in a topic that they couldn't help but be interested also. He was "contagious," they'd say, meaning that he was **charismatic**. He could **get through to them**.

Ross's fellow faculty members were somewhat more divided in their feelings toward him. Some of them were impressed with his energy and dedication and creativity. It was said that he brought a new outlook to his classes, that whenever possible, he tried to teach his students the practical, relevant aspects of history. If they were studying the political system, he would divide the class into political parties. If they studied a famous trial, he might assign one student to be the defendant, others to be the prosecution and defense attorneys, and still others to sit as the jury.

But other faculty members **were more skeptical about Ben**. Some said he was just young, naïve, and overzealous, that after a few years he would calm down and start conducting classes the "right" way—lots of reading, weekly quizzes, classroom lectures. Others simply said they didn't like the way he never wore a suit and tie in class. One or two might even admit they were just plain jealous.

But if there was one thing no teacher had to be jealous

....

charismatic full of energy; interesting and fun

get through to them get his students interested in history and make them understand important events

were more skeptical about Ben did not agree with Ben's way of teaching

of, it was Ben's total inability to cope with film projectors. While perhaps brilliant otherwise, now he only scratched his head and looked at the **tangle of celluloid bunched** in the machine. In just a few minutes his senior history class would arrive, and he had been looking forward to showing them this film for weeks. Why hadn't his teachers' college given a course in film threading?

Ross rolled the film back into its spool and left it **unthreaded**. No doubt one of the kids in his class was some kind of **audiovisual whiz** and could get the machine going in an instant. He walked back to his desk and picked up a pile of homework papers he wanted to distribute to the students before they saw the film.

The marks on the papers had gotten predictable, Ben thought as he thumbed through them. As usual, there were two *A* papers, Laurie Saunders's and Amy Smith's. There was one *A−*, then the normal bunch of *B*'s and *C*'s. There were two *D*'s. One was Brian Ammon, a quarterback on the football team, who seemed to enjoy getting low marks, even though it was obvious to Ben that he had the brains to do much better if he tried. The other *D* was Robert Billings, the class loser. Ross shook his head. The Billings boy was a

....

tangle of celluloid bunched film strip that was stuck
unthreaded next to the machine
audiovisual whiz expert with technology

real problem.

Outside in the hall the bells rang, and Ben heard the sounds of class doors banging open and students **flooding into the corridors**. It was peculiar how students always left class so quickly but somehow arrived at their next class **at the speed of snails**. Generally Ben believed that high school today was a better place for kids to learn than it was when he went. But there were a few things that bothered him. One was his students' lackadaisical attitude about getting to class on time. Sometimes five or even ten minutes of valuable class time would be lost while students straggled in. Back when he was a student, if you weren't in class when the second bell rang, you were in trouble.

The other problem was the homework. Kids just didn't **feel compelled** to do it anymore. You could yell, threaten them with *F*'s or detention, and it didn't matter. Homework had become practically optional. Or, as one of his ninth-graders had told him a few weeks before, "Sure I know homework is important, Mr. Ross, but **my social life** comes first."

Ben chuckled. Social life.

Students were starting to enter the classroom now. Ross

....

flooding into the corridors running out into the halls
at the speed of snails very slowly
feel compelled think they needed
my social life having fun with my friends

spotted David Collins, a tall, good-looking boy who was a running back on the football team. He was also Laurie Saunders's boyfriend.

"David," Ross said, "do you think you could get that film projector set up?"

"Sure thing," David replied.

As Ross watched, David kneeled beside the projector and **went to work nimbly**. In just a few seconds he had it threaded. Ben smiled and thanked him.

Robert Billings trudged into the room. He was a heavy boy with **shirttails perpetually** hanging out and his hair always a mess, as if he never bothered to comb it after getting out of bed in the morning. "We gonna see a movie?" he asked when he saw the projector.

"No, dummy," said a boy named Brad, who especially enjoyed **tormenting him**. "Mr. Ross just likes to set up projectors for fun."

"Okay, Brad," Ben said sternly. "That's enough."

A sufficient number of students had arrived for Ross to start handing out the homework papers. "All right," he said loudly to get the class's attention. "Here are last week's papers. Generally speaking, you did a good job." He walked

....

went to work nimbly quickly started working on it
shirttails perpetually his shirt always
tormenting him making fun of him
A sufficient number of Enough

up and down the aisles passing each paper to its author. "But I'm warning you again. These papers are getting much too sloppy." He stopped and held one up for the class to see. "Look at this. Is it really necessary to **doodle** in the margins of a homework paper?"

The class **tittered**. "Whose is it?" someone asked.

"None of your business." Ben shuffled the papers in his hand and kept handing them out. "From now on, I'm going to start lowering grades on any papers that are really sloppy. If you've made a lot of changes or mistakes on a paper, make a new, neat copy before you hand it in. **Got that?**"

Some members of the class nodded. Others weren't even paying attention. Ben went to the front of the classroom and pulled down the movie screen. It was the third time that semester he'd talked to them about messy homework.

---

doodle draw pictures

tittered laughed quietly

"None of your business." "You do not need to know."

Got that? Do you understand?

BEFORE YOU MOVE ON...

1. **Character** Laurie gives up her free period to work on the school paper. What does this show about her?

2. **Character's Point of View** How do the other teachers feel about Mr. Ross?

LOOK AHEAD Read pages 21–41 to see how students react to the film.

CHAPTER 2

They were studying World War Two, and the film Ben Ross was showing his class that day was a documentary **depicting the atrocities the Nazis committed in their concentration camps**. In the darkened classroom the class stared at the movie screen. They saw emaciated men and women starved so severely that they appeared to be nothing more than skeletons covered with skin. People whose knee joints were the widest parts of their legs.

Ben had already seen this film or films like it half a dozen times. But the sight of such **ruthless inhumane cruelty** by the Nazis still horrified him and made him feel angry. As the film rolled on, he spoke emotionally to the class: "What you are watching took place in Germany

....

depicting the atrocities the Nazis committed in their concentration camps about the way the government tortured and killed Jewish people

ruthless inhumane cruelty evil and brutal treatment

between 1934 and 1945. It was the work of a man named Adolf Hitler, originally a menial laborer, porter, and house painter, who turned to politics after World War One. Germany had been defeated in that war, its leadership was at a low ebb, inflation was high, and thousands were homeless, hungry, and jobless.

"For Hitler it was an opportunity to rise quickly **through the political ranks** of the Nazi Party. He **espoused** the theory that the Jews were the destroyers of civilization and that the Germans were a superior race. Today we know that Hitler was a paranoid, a psychopath, literally a madman. In 1923 he was thrown in jail for his political activities, but by 1934 he and his party had seized control of the German government."

Ben paused for a moment to let the students watch more of the film. They could see the gas chambers now, and the piles of bodies laid out like stove wood. The human skeletons still alive had the gruesome task of stacking the dead under the watching eyes of the Nazi soldiers. Ben felt his stomach churn. How on God's earth could anyone make anyone else do something like that, he asked himself.

He told the students: "The death camps were what

....

through the political ranks to become the leader
espoused believed in

Hitler called his 'Final Solution to the Jewish problem.' But anyone—not just Jews—**deemed** by the Nazis as unfit for their superior race was sent there. They were herded into camps all over Eastern Europe, and once there they were worked, starved, and tortured, and when they couldn't work anymore, they were **exterminated in the gas chambers**. Their remains were disposed of in ovens." Ben paused for a moment and then added: "The life expectancy of the prisoners in the camps was two hundred and seventy days. But many did not survive a week."

On the screen they could see the buildings that housed the ovens. Ben thought of telling the students that the smoke rising from the chimneys above the buildings was from burning human flesh. But he didn't. The experience of watching this film would be awful enough. Thank God man had not invented a way to convey smells through film, because the worst thing of all would have been the stench of it, the stench of the most heinous act ever committed in the history of the human race.

The film was ending and Ben told his students: "In all, the Nazis murdered more than ten million men, women, and children in their extermination camps."

....

deemed decided

exterminated in the gas chambers killed in rooms that sprayed poison on them

The film was over. A student near the door flicked the classroom lights on. As Ben looked around the room, most of the students looked stunned. Ben had not meant to shock them, but he'd known that the film would. Most of these students had grown up in the small, suburban community that spread out lazily around Gordon High. They **were the products of stable, middle-class families**, and despite **the violence-saturated media that permeated society around them**, they were surprisingly naïve and sheltered. Even now a few of the students were starting to fool around. The misery and horror depicted in the film must have seemed to them like just another television program. Robert Billings, sitting near the windows, was asleep with his head buried in his arms on his desk. But near the front of the room, Amy Smith appeared to be wiping a tear out of her eye. Laurie Saunders looked upset too.

"I know many of you are upset," Ben told the class. "But I did not show you this film today just to get an emotional reaction from you. I want you to think about what you saw and what I told you. Does anyone have any questions?"

Amy Smith quickly raised her hand.

"Yes, Amy?"

....

were the products of stable, middle-class families had parents who loved them and had jobs

the violence-saturated media that permeated society around them all the violence they saw on television

"Were all the Germans Nazis?" she asked.

Ben shook his head. "No, as a matter of fact, less than ten percent of the German population belonged to the Nazi Party."

"Then why didn't anyone try to stop them?" Amy asked.

"I can't tell you for sure, Amy," Ross told her. "I can only guess that they were scared. The Nazis might have been a **minority**, but they were a highly organized, armed, and dangerous minority. You have to remember that the rest of the German population was unorganized, and unarmed and frightened. They had also gone through a terrible period of inflation that had virtually ruined their country. Perhaps some of them hoped the Nazis would be able to **restore their society**. Anyway, after the war, the majority of Germans said they didn't know **about the atrocities**."

Near the front of the room, a black youth named Eric raised his hand urgently. "That's crazy," he said. "How could you slaughter ten million people without somebody noticing?"

"Yeah," said Brad, the boy who had picked on Robert Billings before class began. "That can't be true."

It was obvious to Ben that the film had affected a large

....

minority small group

restore their society create new jobs for them and make the country powerful and strong again

about the atrocities that the Nazis tortured and killed millions of people

part of the class, and he was pleased. It was good to see them concerned about something. "Well," he said to Eric and Brad, "I can only tell you that after the war the Germans claimed they knew nothing of the concentration camps or the killings."

Now Laurie Saunders raised her hand. "But Eric's right," she said. "How could the Germans **sit back** while the Nazis **slaughtered people all around them** and say they didn't know about it? How could they do that? How could they even say that?"

"All I can tell you," Ben said, "is that the Nazis were highly organized and feared. The behavior of the rest of the German population is a mystery—why they didn't try to stop it, how they could say they didn't know. We just don't know the answers."

Eric's hand was up again. "All I can say is, I would never let such a small minority of people **rule the majority**."

"Yeah," said Brad. "I wouldn't let a couple of Nazis scare me into pretending I didn't see or hear anything."

There were other hands raised with questions, but before Ben could call on anyone, the bell rang out and the class was rushing out into the hall.

....

sit back not do anything

slaughtered people all around them killed millions of people as if they were animals

rule the majority take control of an entire country

David Collins stood up. His stomach was grumbling like mad. That morning he'd gotten up late and had to skip his usual three-course breakfast to make it to school on time. Even though the film Mr. Ross had shown really bothered him, he couldn't help thinking that next period was lunch.

He looked over at Laurie Saunders, his girlfriend, who was still sitting in her seat. "Come on, Laurie," he urged her. "We have to get down to the cafeteria fast. You know how long the line gets."

But Laurie waved him to go without her. "I'll catch up later."

David scowled. He was **torn between** waiting for his girlfriend and filling his growling stomach. The stomach won, and David took off down the hall.

After he was gone, Laurie got up from her seat and looked at Mr. Ross. There were only a couple of kids left in the room now. And except for Robert Billings, who was just waking up from his nap, they were the ones who seemed the most disturbed about the film. "I can't even believe that all the Nazis were that cruel," Laurie told her teacher. "I don't believe anyone could be that cruel."

Ben nodded. "After the war, many Nazis tried to

....

torn between had to decide between

excuse their behavior by claiming they were only following orders and that they would have been killed themselves if they hadn't."

Laurie shook her head. "No, that's no excuse. They could have run away. They could have fought back. They had their own eyes and their own minds. They could think for themselves. Nobody would *just* follow an order like that."

"But that's what they said," Ben told her.

Laurie shook her head again. "It's sick," she said, her voice filled with revulsion. "Just totally sick."

Ben could only nod in agreement.

Robert Billings was trying to sneak past Ben's desk.

"Robert," Ben said. "Wait a minute."

The boy froze, but could not look his teacher in the eye.

"Are you getting enough sleep at home?" Ben asked.

Robert nodded dumbly.

Ben sighed. All semester he had been trying to **get through to** this boy. He couldn't stand seeing him picked on by the other students and it dismayed him that Robert didn't at least try to participate in class. "Robert," his teacher said sternly, "if you don't start participating in this class I

....

excuse their behavior by claiming they were only following orders say that it was not their fault so many people died because they were doing what their leader told them to do

get through to connect with; relate to

will have to fail you. You'll never graduate at this rate."

Robert glanced at his teacher and then looked away again.

"Don't you have anything to say?" Ben asked.

Robert shrugged. "I don't care," he said.

"What do you mean you don't care?" Ben asked.

Robert took a few steps toward the door. Ben could see that he was uncomfortable about being questioned. "Robert?"

The boy stopped, but he still could not look at his teacher. "I wouldn't do any good anyway," he mumbled.

Ben wondered what he could say. Robert's case was a tough one: the younger brother **wallowing in the shadow of an** older brother who had been the **quintessential model student and big man on campus**. Jeff Billings had been an all-conference pitcher in high school and was now in the Baltimore Orioles **farm system** while he studied medicine in the off season. In school he'd been a straight *A* student who excelled at everything he did. The kind of guy even Ben had despised in high school.

Seeing that he could never compete with his brother's achievements, Robert had apparently decided it was better

....

wallowing in the shadow of an feeling not as smart as his

quintessential model student and big man on campus
perfect student with a lot of friends

farm system minor league baseball organization

not even to try.

"Listen, Robert," Ben said, "no one expects you to be **another Jeff Billings**."

Robert glanced quickly at Ben and then started chewing nervously on his thumbnail.

"All we're asking is that you try," Ben said.

"I have to go," Robert said, looking down at the floor.

"I don't even care about sports, Robert," Ben said. But the boy had already begun to move slowly toward the door.

....

another Jeff Billings just like your older brother

CHAPTER 3

David Collins was sitting in the outdoor **courtyard** next to the cafeteria. He had already **wolfed down** half his lunch by the time Laurie arrived, and he was beginning to feel like a normal human being again. He watched Laurie put her tray down next to his and then noticed that Robert Billings was also headed for the courtyard.

"Hey, look," David whispered as Laurie sat down. They watched as Robert stepped out of the cafeteria carrying a tray, looking for a place to eat. **True to form**, he had already started eating and stood in the doorway with half a hot dog sticking out of his mouth.

There were two girls from Mr. Ross's history class sitting

....

courtyard area with tables
wolfed down quickly eaten
True to form Like he did everyday

at the table Robert chose. As Robert set his tray down, they both stood up and took their trays to another table. Robert pretended he hadn't noticed.

David shook his head. "Gordon High's very own **Untouchable**," he mumbled.

"Do you think there's something really wrong with him?" Laurie asked.

David shrugged. "I don't know. He's been pretty strange for as long as I can remember. Then again, if people treated me like that, I'd probably be pretty strange too. It's just weird that he and his brother could come from the same family."

"Did I ever tell you that my mother knows his mother?" Laurie asked.

"His mother ever talk about him?" David asked.

"No. Except I think she told me once that they had him tested and he really does have a normal **I.Q.** He's not really dumb or anything."

"Just weird," David said and went back to eating his lunch. But Laurie only picked at hers. She seemed **preoccupied**.

"What is it?" David asked.

....

Untouchable outsider; person nobody likes
I.Q. Intelligence Quotient; intelligence level
preoccupied to be thinking about something else

"That film, David," Laurie answered. "It really **bothers** me. Doesn't it bother you?"

David thought for a moment. Then he said, "Yeah, sure, as something horrible that happened once, it bothers me. But that was a long time ago, Laurie. To me it's like **a piece of history**. You can't change what happened then."

"But you can't forget it," Laurie said. She tried a bite of her hamburger, then made a face and put it down.

"Well, you can't go around being **bummed out** about it for the rest of your life either," David said. He **eyed** Laurie's uneaten hamburger. "By the way, you gonna eat that?"

Laurie shook her head. The movie had left her without much of an appetite. "Help yourself."

Not only did David help himself to her burger, he finished off her fries, salad, and ice cream as well. Laurie looked in his direction, but her eyes were distant.

"Hmm." David wiped his lips with a napkin.

"Would you like anything more?" Laurie asked.

"Well, to tell you the truth . . ."

"Hey, is this seat taken?" someone behind them said.

"I was here first!" said another voice.

David and Laurie looked up to find Amy Smith and

....

bothers upsets
a piece of history something that doesn't affect me
bummed out depressed
eyed looked at

Brian Ammon, **the quarterback**, both heading for their table from opposite directions.

"What do you mean you were here first?" Brian asked.

"Well, I meant I wanted to be here first," Amy replied.

"Meaning to be first doesn't count," Brian said. "Besides, I have to talk to Dave about football."

"And I have to talk to Laurie," Amy said.

"What about?" Brian asked.

"Well, about keeping her company while you talk about boring football."

"Stop it," Laurie said. "There's room for two."

"But with them you need room for three," Amy said, nodding at Brian and David.

"**Hardy har har**," Brian grunted.

David and Laurie slid over, and Amy and Brian squeezed in next to them at the table. Amy was right about room for three—Brian was carrying two full lunch trays.

"Hey, what are you doing with all this food?" David asked, patting Brian on the back. Although he was the team's quarterback, Brian was not very big. David **stood a full head** taller than him.

"I gotta gain some weight," Brian said as he started to

....

the quarterback a football player
Hardy har har You are not funny
stood a full head was a lot

wolf down his lunch. "I'm gonna need every pound I've got against **those guys** from Clarkstown on Saturday. They are big. I mean, huge. I hear they got a linebacker who **stands six three** and weighs two-twenty."

"I don't see what you're worried about," Amy said. "No one that heavy can run very fast."

Brian rolled his eyes. "He doesn't *have* to run, Amy. All he has to do is squash quarterbacks."

"Will you have a chance on Saturday?" Laurie asked. She was thinking about the story they would need for *The Grapevine.*

David shrugged. "I don't know. The team's pretty disorganized. We're way behind on learning our plays and stuff. Half the guys don't even show up for practice."

"Yeah," Brian agreed. "Coach Schiller said he was gonna throw anyone who didn't show up for practice off the team. But if he did that we wouldn't even have enough guys to play."

No one seemed to have anything more to say about football, so Brian bit into his second hamburger.

David's thoughts **drifted to** other pressing matters. "Hey, is anyone here good at **calculus**?"

....

those guys the other team; our opponents
stands six three is six feet and three inches tall
drifted to moved onto
calculus math

"Why are you taking calculus?" Amy asked.

"You need it **for engineering**," David said.

"So why not wait till college?" Brian asked.

"I heard it was so hard you have to take it twice to understand it," David explained. "So I figured I'd take it once now and once later."

Amy nudged Laurie. "I think your boyfriend is strange," she said.

"Talk about strange," Brian whispered, nodding toward Robert Billings.

They all looked. Robert was sitting alone at his table, **engrossed in a Spider-Man** comic book. His lips moved as he read and there was a red streak of catsup on his chin.

"You see him sleep through the whole movie?" Brian asked.

"Don't remind Laurie," David told him. "She's upset."

"What, about that movie?" Brian asked.

Laurie gave David a dirty look. "Do you *have* to tell everybody?"

"Well, it's true, isn't it?" David asked.

"Oh, just leave me alone," Laurie answered.

"I can understand how you feel," Amy told her. "I

---

for engineering to get a job designing and building machines and engines

engrossed in a Spider-Man reading a superhero

thought it was just awful."

Laurie turned to David. "There, you see? I'm not the only one that it bothered."

"Hey," David said defensively. "I didn't say I wasn't bothered by it. I just said it's over now. Forget about it. It happened once and the world learned its lesson. It'll never happen again."

"I hope not," Laurie said, picking up her tray.

"Where're you going?" David asked her.

"I have to go work on *The Grapevine*," Laurie said.

"Wait," Amy said, "I'll go with you."

David and Brian watched the two girls go.

"Gee, she really is upset about that movie, isn't she?" Brian said.

"Yeah." David nodded. "You know, she always takes **stuff like that** too seriously."

Amy Smith and Laurie Saunders sat in *The Grapevine* office talking. Amy wasn't on the newspaper staff, but she often **hung out** with Laurie in the publications office. The office door could be locked, and Amy would sit inside by an open window, holding a cigarette outside and blowing the

....

stuff like that history and politics
hung out stayed

smoke out. If a teacher came in, she could drop the cigarette to the ground and there would hardly be any smell of smoke in the room.

"That was an awful movie," Amy said.

Laurie nodded quietly.

"Are you and David having a fight?" her friend asked.

"Oh, not really." Laurie couldn't help smiling slightly. "I just wish he would take something besides football seriously. He's—I don't know—he's **such a jock** sometimes."

"But he gets good grades," Amy said. "At least he's not a **dumb jock** like Brian."

The two girls giggled for a moment and then Amy asked, "Why does he want to be an engineer? It sounds so boring."

"He wants to **be a computer engineer**," Laurie said. "Did you ever see the one he has at home? He built it from a kit."

"Somehow I missed it," Amy said **facetiously**. "By the way, have you decided what you're doing next year?"

Laurie shook her head. "Maybe we'll go somewhere together. It depends on where we get accepted."

"Your parents will be thrilled," Amy said.

"I don't think they'd mind that much," Laurie said.

....

such a jock only interested in sports
dumb jock athlete who does not care about school
be a computer engineer work with computers
facetiously sarcastically; not seriously

"Why don't you just get married?" Amy asked.

Laurie made a face. "Oh, Amy. I mean, I guess I love David, but who wants to get married yet?"

Amy smiled. "Oh, I don't know, if David asked *me* I might consider it," she teased.

Laurie laughed. "Would you like me to **drop a hint**?"

"Come off it, Laurie," Amy said. "You know how much he likes you. He doesn't even look at other girls."

"He'd better not," Laurie said. She noticed that there was a wistful note to Amy's voice. Ever since Laurie had started dating David, Amy had wanted to date a football player too. It sometimes bothered Laurie that **underlying their friendship** was a constant competition for boys, grades, popularity, almost everything one could compete for. Even though they were best friends, that constant competition somehow prevented them from being really close.

Suddenly there was a loud knock on the door and someone tried **the doorknob**. Both girls jumped. "Who is it?" Laurie asked.

"Principal Owens," a deep voice replied. "Why is this door locked?"

Amy's eyes went wide with fear. She quickly

....

drop a hint let him know
underlying their friendship it seemed like there
the doorknob to open it

dropped her cigarette and started **digging through her pocketbook** for a stick of gum or a mint.

"Uh, it must have been an accident," Laurie replied nervously, going to the door.

"Well, open it immediately!"

Amy looked terrified.

Laurie gave her a helpless look and pulled the door open.

Outside in the hall were Carl Block, *The Grapevine's* investigative reporter, and Alex Cooper, the music reviewer. They were both grinning.

"Oh, you two!" Laurie said angrily. Behind her Amy looked like she was going to faint as the two **biggest practical jokers in the school** stepped into the room.

Carl was a tall, thin guy with blond hair. Alex, who was stocky and dark, was wearing earphones connected to a small tape player. "Something illegal going on in here?" Carl asked slyly, making his eyebrows bounce up and down.

"You made me waste a perfectly good cigarette," Amy complained.

"Tisk, tisk," Alex said, looking on disapprovingly.

"So how is the paper coming?" Carl asked.

"What do you mean?" Laurie asked **in exasperation**.

....

digging through her pocketbook looking in her bag

biggest practical jokers in school boys who always made jokes

in exasperation with frustration

"Neither of you has handed in your assignments for this issue."

"Oh-oh." Alex was suddenly looking at his watch and backing away toward the door. "I just remembered I have to **catch a plane to Argentina**."

"I'll drive you to the airport!" Carl said, following him out the door.

Laurie looked at Amy and shook her head wearily. "Those two," she mumbled, making a fist.

....

catch a plane to Argentina be somewhere else

BEFORE YOU MOVE ON...

1. **Cause and Effect** Mr. Ross shows a film about the Holocaust in class. How do his students respond?

2. **Character's Point of View** Reread pages 28–29. Robert does not think he should even try in school. Why?

LOOK AHEAD Read pages 42–62 to see what lesson Mr. Ross has planned.

CHAPTER 4

Something bothered Ben Ross. He couldn't quite put his finger on it, but he was **intrigued by** the questions the kids in his history class had asked him after the film that day. It made him wonder. Why hadn't he been able to give the students adequate answers to their questions? Was the behavior of the majority of Germans during the Nazi **regime** really so **inexplicable**?

That afternoon before he left school, Ross had stopped at the library and taken out an armful of books. His wife, Christy, would be playing tennis that evening with some friends, so he knew he would have a long period of uninterrupted time to **pursue his thoughts**. Now, several hours later, after reading through a number of books, Ben

....

intrigued by interested in
regime rule
inexplicable hard to explain
pursue his thoughts think and research

suspected that he would not find the real answer written anywhere. It made him wonder. Was this something historians knew **words could not explain**? Was it something one could only understand by being there? Or, if possible, by **re-creating a similar situation**?

The idea intrigued Ross. Suppose, he thought, just suppose he took a period, perhaps two periods, and tried an experiment. Just tried to give his students a sampling, a taste of what life in Nazi Germany might have been like. If he could just figure out how it could be done, how the experiment could be run, he was certain it would make far more of an impression on the students than any book explanation could ever make. It certainly was worth a try.

Christy Ross didn't get in that night until after eleven o'clock. She'd played tennis and then had dinner with a friend. She got home to find her husband sitting at their kitchen table surrounded by books.

"Doing your homework?"

"In a way, yes," Ben Ross replied without looking up from his books.

On top of one of the books Christy noticed an empty

....

words could not explain would not make sense to people who had not lived in Germany at the time

re-creating a similar situation creating an experiment that would put a few people in control of many people

glass and an empty plate with a few crumbs from what once must have been a sandwich.

"Well, at least you remembered to feed yourself," she said, picking up the dish and placing it in the sink.

Her husband didn't answer. **His nose was still stuck in** the book.

"I **bet you're just dying to find out** how badly I beat Betty Lewis tonight," she said, kidding him.

Ben looked up. "What?"

"I said I beat Betty Lewis tonight," Christy told him.

Her husband had a blank look on his face.

Christy laughed. "Betty Lewis. You know, the Betty Lewis who I've never won more than two games in a set from. I beat her tonight. In two sets. Six-four; seven-five."

"Oh, uh, that's very good," Ben said **absently**. He looked back down at the book and started reading again.

Someone else might have been offended by his apparent rudeness, but Christy wasn't. She knew Ben was the kind of person who got involved with things. Not just involved, but utterly absorbed in them to the point where he tended to forget that the rest of the world existed. She'd never forget the time in graduate school when he got interested in

....

His nose was still stuck in He was still reading

bet you're just dying to find out know you really want me to tell you

absently but was not really paying attention

American Indians. For months he was so **wrapped up in** Indians that he forgot about the rest of his life. On weekends he'd visit Indian reservations or spend hours looking for old books in dusty libraries. He even started bringing Indians home for dinner! And wearing deerskin moccasins! Christy used to get up some mornings wondering if he was going to **put on war paint**.

But that was the way Ben was. One summer she'd taught him to play **bridge**, and within a month not only was he a better bridge player than she, but he was driving her crazy, insisting that they play bridge every minute of the day. He only calmed down after he won a local bridge tournament and ran out of worthy competitors. It was almost frightening, the way he lost himself in each new adventure.

Christy looked at the books scattered about the kitchen table and sighed. "What is it this time?" she asked. "The Indians again? Astronomy? The **behavioral characteristics** of killer whales?"

When her husband didn't answer, she picked up some of the books. *"The Rise and Fall of the Third Reich? Hitler's Youth?"* She frowned. "What are you doing, cramming for a degree in dictatorship?"

....

wrapped up in fascinated with; interested in
put on war paint paint his face like a warrior
bridge a card game
behavioral characteristics way of life; habits

"Not funny," Ben muttered without looking up.

"You're right," Christy admitted.

Ben Ross sat back and looked at his wife. "One of my students asked me a question today that I couldn't answer."

"So what else is new?" Christy asked.

"But I don't think I ever saw the answer written anywhere," Ben told her. "It just may be an answer they have to learn for themselves."

Christy Ross nodded. "Well, I can see what kind of night this is going to be," she said. "Just remember, tomorrow you have to be awake enough to teach an entire day of classes."

Her husband nodded. "I know, I know."

Christy Ross bent down and kissed him on his forehead. "Try not to wake me. *If* you come to sleep tonight."

CHAPTER 5

The next day the students drifted in slowly as usual. Some took their seats, others stood around talking. Robert Billings was by the windows, tying knots in the blind cords. While he was doing that, Brad, **his incessant tormentor**, walked past and patted him on the back, sticking a **small sign that said "kick me"** to his shirt.

It looked like just another typical day in history class until the kids noticed that their teacher had written in large letters across the blackboard: STRENGTH THROUGH DISCIPLINE.

"What's that supposed to mean?" someone asked.

"I'll tell you just as soon as you're all seated," Ben Ross answered. When the kids were all in their places, he

---

his incessant tormentor who constantly bullied him

small sign that said "kick me" note so other kids would laugh at him

began to lecture. "Today I am going to talk to you about **discipline**."

A collective groan went up from the seated students. There were some teachers whose classes you knew would be a drag, but most of the students expected Ross's history class to be pretty good—which meant no dumb lectures on stuff like discipline.

"Hold it," Ben told them. "Before you make a judgment, give this a chance. It could be exciting."

"Oh sure," someone said.

"Oh sure is right," Ben told his students. "Now when I talk about discipline, I'm talking about power," he said, making a fist to **accentuate** the point. "And I'm talking about success. Success through discipline. Is there anyone here who isn't interested in power and success?"

"Probably Robert," Brad said. A bunch of kids **snickered**.

"Now wait," Ben told them. "David, Brian, Eric, you play football. You already know it takes discipline to win."

"That must be why we haven't won a game in two years," Eric said, and the class laughed.

It took their teacher a few moments to calm them

....

discipline self control; restrictions
accentuate emphasize
snickered laughed

down again. "Listen," he said, **gesturing** toward a pretty, red-haired student who appeared to be sitting taller in her chair than those around her. "Andrea, you're a ballet dancer. Doesn't it take ballet dancers long, hard hours of work to develop their skills?"

She nodded, and Ross turned to the rest of the class. "It's the same with every art. Painting, writing, music—all of them take years of hard work and discipline to master. Hard work, discipline, and control."

"So what?" said a student who was **slouching down** in his chair.

"So what?" Ben asked. "I'll show you. Suppose I could prove to you that you can create power through discipline. Suppose we could do it right here in this classroom. What would you say to that?"

Ross had expected another **wisecrack**, and he was surprised when it didn't come. Instead the students were becoming interested and curious. Ben went behind his desk and pulled his wooden chair in front of the room so that all the students could see it.

"All right," he said. "Discipline begins with posture. Amy, come up here for a minute."

....

gesturing pointing
slouching down sitting low
wisecrack negative comment; joke

As Amy rose, Brian mumbled, "**Teacher's pet**." Normally that would have been enough to start the entire class laughing, but only a few chuckled. The rest ignored him. Everyone was wondering what their teacher was up to.

As Amy sat in the chair at the front of the room, Ben instructed her on how to sit. "Place your hands flat across the small of your back and force your spine straight up. There, can't you breathe more easily?"

Around the classroom, many of the students were imitating the position they saw Amy taking. But even though they were sitting straighter, some couldn't help finding it humorous. David was the next to try his hand at a joke: "Is this history, or did I come to **phys ed** by mistake?" he asked. A few kids laughed, but still tried to improve their posture.

"Come on, David," Ben said. "Give it a try. We've had enough **wise-guy** remarks."

Grudgingly David pushed himself up straight in his chair. Meanwhile their teacher walked down each aisle, checking the posture of each student. It was amazing, Ross thought. Somehow he'd **hooked them**. Why, even Robert . . .

....

Teacher's pet His favorite student
phys ed physical education; gym class
wise-guy unnecessary
hooked them got them to listen and be interested

"Class," Ben announced, "I want everyone to see how Robert's legs are **parallel**. His ankles are locked, his knees are bent at ninety degrees. See how straight his spine is. Chin tucked in, head up. That's very good, Robert."

Robert, the class nerd, looked up at his teacher and smiled briefly, then returned to his stiff upright position. Around the room the other students tried to copy him.

Ben returned to the front of the classroom. "All right. Now I want you all to get up and walk around the room. When I give the command, I want you to return to your seats as quickly as possible and assume the proper seating posture. Come on, everyone, up, up, up."

The students stood up and started wandering around the room. Ben knew he couldn't let them go too long or they'd lose their concentration on the exercise, so he quickly said, "Take your seats!"

The students dashed back to their seats. There were bumps and grunts as a few ran into each other, and around the room some kids laughed, but the **dominant** sound was the loud scraping of chair legs as the kids sat down.

In the front of the room, Ben shook his head. "That was the most disorganized mess I've ever seen. This isn't

parallel straight and at the same distant apart
dominant main, loudest

duck, duck, goose, this is an experiment in movement and posture. Now come on, let's try it again. This time without the chatter. The quicker and more controlled you are, the faster you will be able to reach your seats properly. Okay? Now, everyone, up!"

For the next twenty minutes the class practiced getting out of their seats, wandering around in **apparent disorganization** and then, at their teacher's command, quickly returning to their seats and the correct seated posture. Ben shouted orders more like a **drill sergeant** than a teacher. Once they seemed to have **mastered** quick and correct seating, he threw in a new twist. They would still leave their seats and return. But now they would return from the hallway and Ross would time them with a stopwatch.

On the first try, it took forty-eight seconds. The second time they were able to do it in half a minute. Before the last attempt, David had an idea.

"Listen," he told his classmates as they stood outside in the hall waiting for Mr. Ross's signal. "Let's line up in the order of who has to go the farthest to reach their desks inside. That way we won't have to bump into each other."

....

duck, duck, goose a little kid's game
apparent disorganization confusion
drill sergeant person who trains soldiers
mastered gotten very good at

The rest of the class agreed. As they got into the correct order, they couldn't help noticing that Robert was at the head of the line. "The new **head of the class**," someone whispered as they waited nervously for their teacher to give them the sign. Ben snapped his fingers and the column of students moved quickly and quietly into the room. As the last student reached his seat, Ben clicked the stopwatch off. He was smiling. "Sixteen seconds."

The class cheered.

"All right, all right, **quiet down**," their teacher said, returning to the front of the room. To his surprise, the students calmed down quickly. The silence that suddenly filled the room was almost eerie. Normally the only time the room was that still, Ross thought, was when it was empty.

"Now, there are three more rules that you must obey," he told them. "One. Everybody must have pencils and note paper for note-taking. Two. When asking or answering a question, you must stand **at the side of** your seats. And three. The first words you say when answering or asking a question are, 'Mr. Ross.' All right?"

Around the room, heads nodded.

....

head of the class leader
quiet down everybody be quiet
at the side of next to

"All right," Mr. Ross said. "Brad, who was the British Prime Minister before Churchill?"

Still sitting at his seat, Brad chewed nervously on a fingernail. "Uh, wasn't it—"

But before he could say more, Mr. Ross quickly cut him off. "Wrong, Brad, you already forgot the rules I just told you." He looked across the room at Robert. "Robert, show Brad the **proper procedure for** answering a question."

Instantly Robert stood up next to his desk **at attention**. "Mr. Ross."

"Correct," Mr. Ross said. "Thank you, Robert."

"Aw, this is dumb," Brad mumbled.

"Just because you couldn't do it right," someone said.

"Brad," Mr. Ross said, "who was the Prime Minister before Churchill?"

This time Brad rose and stood beside his desk. "Mr. Ross, it was, uh, Prime Minister, uh."

"You're still too slow, Brad," Mr. Ross said. "From now on, everyone make your answers as short as possible, and spit them out when asked. Now, Brad, try again."

This time Brad **snapped up** beside his seat. "Mr. Ross, Chamberlain."

....

proper procedure for correct method to use when
at attention quickly and ready to answer
snapped up stood up quickly

Ben nodded approvingly. "Now that's the way to answer a question. **Punctual, precise, with punch.** Andrea, what country did Hitler invade in September of 1939?"

Andrea, the ballet dancer, stood stiffly by her desk. "Mr. Ross, I don't know."

Mr. Ross smiled. "Still, a good response because you used proper form. Amy, do you know the answer?"

Amy hopped up beside her desk. "Mr. Ross, Poland."

"Excellent," Mr. Ross said. "Brian, what was the name of Hitler's political party?"

Brian quickly got out of his chair. "Mr. Ross, the Nazis."

Mr. Ross nodded. "That's good, Brian. Very quick. Now, does anyone know the official name of the party? Laurie?"

Laurie Saunders stood up beside her desk. "The National Socialist—"

"No!" There was a sharp bang as Mr. Ross struck his desktop with a ruler. "Now do it again correctly."

Laurie sat down, a confused look on her face. What had she done wrong? David leaned over and whispered in her ear. Oh, right. She stood up again. "Mr. Ross, the National Socialist German Workers' Party."

....

Punctual, precise, with punch. Quickly, correctly, and with power.

"Correct," Mr. Ross replied.

Mr. Ross kept asking questions, and around the room students jumped to attention, eager to show that they knew both the answer and the correct form with which to give it. It was **a far cry** from the normally casual atmosphere of the classroom, but neither Ben nor his students reflected on that fact. They were too caught up in this new game. The speed and precision of each question and answer were exhilarating. Soon Ben was perspiring as he shouted each question out and another student rose sharply beside his or her desk to shout back a terse reply.

"Peter, who proposed the Lend-Lease Act?"

"Mr. Ross, Roosevelt."

"Right. Eric, who died in the death camps?"

"Mr. Ross, the Jews."

"Anyone else, Brad?"

"Mr. Ross, **gypsies, homosexuals, and the feeble-minded**."

"Good. Amy, why were they murdered?"

"Mr. Ross, because they weren't part of the superior race."

"Correct. David, who ran the death camps?"

....

a far cry very different

gypsies, homosexuals, and the feeble-minded people without homes, people who loved others of the same sex, and old, sick people

"Mr. Ross, the **S.S.**"

"Excellent!"

Out in the hall, the bells were ringing, but no one in the classroom moved from their seat. Still carried by the **momentum** of the class's progress that period, Ben stood at the front of the room and issued the final order of the day. "Tonight, finish reading chapter seven and read the first half of chapter eight. That's all, class dismissed." Before him the class rose in what seemed like a single movement and rushed out into the hall.

"Wow, that was weird, man, it was like a rush," Brian **gasped in uncharacteristic enthusiasm**. He and some of the students from Mr. Ross's class were standing in a tight pack in the corridor, still **riding on** the energy they'd felt in the classroom.

"I've never felt anything like that before," said Eric beside him.

"Well, it sure beats taking notes," Amy cracked.

"Yeah," Brian said. He and a couple of other students laughed.

"Hey, but don't knock it," David said. "That was really

....

S.S. Nazi military police
momentum energy
gasped in uncharacteristic enthusiasm said excitedly
riding on feeling

different. It was like, when we all acted together, we were more than just a class. We were a unit. Remember what Mr. Ross said about power? I think he was right. Didn't you feel it?"

"Aw, you're taking it too seriously," said Brad behind him.

"Yeah?" David said. "Well then, how do you explain it?"

Brad shrugged. "What's to explain? Ross asked questions, we answered them. It was like any other class except we had to sit up straight and stand next to our desks. I think you're making **a big deal out of nothing**."

"I don't know, Brad," David said as he turned and left the pack of students.

"Where're you going?" Brian asked.

"The **john**," David answered. "**Catch up to** you in the cafeteria."

"Okay," Brian said.

"Hey, remember to sit up straight," Brad said, and the others laughed.

David pushed through the door to the men's room. He really wasn't sure if Brad was right or not. Maybe he was making a big deal out of nothing, but on the other hand,

....

a big deal out of nothing this into something more serious when it was just a simple experiment

john bathroom

Catch up to I'll meet

there had been that feeling, that group unity. Maybe it didn't make that much difference in the classroom. After all, you were just answering questions. But suppose you took that group feeling, that high energy feeling, and got the football team into it. There were some good athletes on the team, it made David mad that they **had such a bad record**. They really weren't that bad—they **were just undermotivated and disorganized**. David knew that if he could ever get the team even half as charged up as Mr. Ross's history class had been that day, they could **tear apart** most of the teams in their league.

Inside the john, David heard the second bell ring, warning students that the next period was about to begin. He stepped out of a stall and was heading to the sinks when he saw someone and stopped abruptly. The bathroom had emptied out and only one person was left, Robert. He was standing in front of a mirror, tucking in his shirt, unaware that he wasn't alone. As David watched, the class loser straightened some of the hair on his head and stared at his reflection. Then he snapped to attention and his lips moved silently, as if he was still in Mr. Ross's class answering questions.

....

had such a bad record lost so many games

were just undermotivated and disorganized just did not care enough to win and were not organized

tear apart beat, defeat

David stood motionless as Robert practiced the move again. And again.

Late that night in their bedroom, Christy Ross sat on the side of the bed in her red nightgown and brushed her long **auburn** hair. Near her Ben was pulling his pajamas out of a drawer. "You know," he said, "I would have thought they'd all hate it, being ordered around and forced to sit straight and recite answers. Instead they **took to it** like they'd been waiting for something like this their whole lives. It was weird."

"Don't you think they were just playing it like a game?" Christy asked. "Simply competing with each other to see who could be the fastest and straightest?"

"I'm sure that was part of it," Ben told his wife. "But even a game is something you either choose to play or not to play. They didn't have to play that game, but they wanted to. The strangest thing was, once we started I could **feel them wanting more**. They wanted to be disciplined. And each time they mastered one discipline, they wanted another. When the bell rang at the end of the period and they were still in their seats, I knew it meant more to them

....

auburn reddish brown

took to it followed my orders

feel them wanting more tell that they wanted to continue and wanted more rules than just a game."

Christy stopped brushing her hair. "You mean they stayed *after* the bell?" she asked.

Ben nodded. "That's what I mean."

His wife looked at him skeptically but then grinned. "Ben, I think you've **created a monster**."

"**Hardly**," Ben replied, chuckling.

Christy put down her brush and rubbed some cream into her face. On his side of the bed, Ben was pulling on his pajama top. Christy was waiting for her husband to lean over for their **customary** goodnight kiss. But tonight it was not forthcoming. He was still lost in thought.

"Ben?" Christy said.

"Yeah?"

"Do you think you'll go on with it tomorrow?"

"I don't think so," her husband replied. "We've got to get on to the Japanese campaign."

Christy closed the jar of cream and settled comfortably into the bed. But on his side Ben still had not moved. He had told his wife how surprisingly enthusiastic his students had been that afternoon, but he had not told her that he too had gotten caught up in it. It would almost be embarrassing

....

created a monster changed your students into strange animals

Hardly I do not think so

customary routine, daily

to admit that he could get swept up in such a simple game. But yet **on reflection** he knew that he had. The **fierce exchange** of questions and answers, the quest for perfect discipline—**it had been infectious and, in a way, mesmerizing**. He had enjoyed his students' accomplishment. Interesting, he thought as he got into bed.

....

on reflection looking back; thinking about that day

fierce exchange fast and intense time

it had been infectious and, in a way, mesmerizing the feeling of power and energy was felt by everyone, and it felt amazing

BEFORE YOU MOVE ON...

1. **Character's Motive** Reread pages 42–43. Why does Mr. Ross decide to use his students in an experiment?

2. **Conflict** Reread pages 57–60. The students respond to the experiment positively. Why?

LOOK AHEAD Read pages 63–80 to see if the students continue the experiment.

CHAPTER 6

For Ben, what happened the next day was extremely unusual. Instead of his students **straggling into** class after the bell had rung, it was he who was late. He'd accidentally left his lecture notes and book on Japan in his car that morning and had to run out to the parking lot before class to get them. As he rushed into the classroom he expected to find **a madhouse**, but he was in for a surprise.

In his room were five neat rows of desks, seven desks to a row. At each desk a student sat stiffly in the posture Ben had taught them the previous day. The room was silent, and Ross **surveyed** his class uneasily. Was it a joke? Here and there he saw a face on the verge of smiling, but those were clearly outnumbered by faces at stiff attention, staring

....

straggling into coming late to
a madhouse his students talking and misbehaving
surveyed looked over

straight ahead, concentrating. A few students glanced at him uncertainly—waiting to see if he'd carry it further. Should he? It was such an experience and so different from **the norm that it tantalized him**. What could they learn from this? What could he learn? **Tempted by the unknown,** Ben decided it was worth finding out.

"Well, okay," he said, putting away his notes. "What's going on here?"

The students looked at him uncertainly.

Ben looked toward the far side of the room. "Robert?"

Robert Billings quickly rose beside his desk. His shirt was tucked in and his hair was combed. "Mr. Ross, discipline."

"Yes, discipline," Mr. Ross agreed. "But that's just part of it. There's something more." Then he turned to the blackboard, and underneath the large "STRENGTH THROUGH DISCIPLINE" from the day before, he added, "COMMUNITY."

He turned back to the class. "Community is the bond between people who work and struggle together for a common goal. It's like building a barn with your neighbors."

A few students in the room chuckled. But David knew

....

the norm that it tantalized him what class was usually like that he thought about continuing the experiment

Tempted by the unknown, Wanting to see what would happen,

what Mr. Ross was saying. It was what he'd thought about yesterday after class. It was the kind of **team spirit** the football team needed.

"It's the feeling that you're part of something that's more important than yourself," Mr. Ross was telling them. "You're a movement, a team, a cause. You're committed to something—"

"I think we ought to be committed all right," someone mumbled, but the nearby students **hushed him**.

"Like discipline," Mr. Ross continued, "to understand community fully you have to experience it and participate in it. From now on, our two **mottos** will be, 'Strength Through Discipline' and 'Strength Through Community.' Everyone, repeat our mottos."

Around the room, students rose beside their desks and recited the slogans: "Strength Through Discipline, Strength Through Community."

A few students, including Laurie and Brad, did not join them, but sat uncomfortably in their chairs as Mr. Ross had the class repeat the mottos again. Finally Laurie rose, and then Brad. Now the entire class stood beside their desks.

"What we need now is a symbol for our new

....

team spirit group effort
hushed him told him to be quiet
mottos sayings we believe in

community," Mr. Ross told them. He turned back to the board and, after a moment's thought, drew a circle with the outline of a wave inside it. "This will be our symbol. A wave is a pattern of change. It has movement, direction, and impact. From now on, our community, our movement will be known as The Wave." He paused and looked at the class standing at stiff attention, accepting everything he told them. "And this will be our **salute**," he said, cupping his right hand in the shape of a wave, then tapping it against his left shoulder and holding it upright "Class, give the salute," he ordered.

The class gave the salute. Some hit their right shoulders instead of their left. Others forgot to hit their shoulders **entirely**. "Again," Ross ordered, making the salute himself. He repeated the exercise until everyone had it right.

"All right," their teacher said when they'd gotten it. Once again the class could feel the **resurgence** of power and unity that had overwhelmed them the day before. "This is our salute and our salute only," he told them. "Whenever you see another Wave member, you will salute. Robert, salute and give our mottos."

Standing stiffly beside his seat, Robert performed the

....

salute greeting
entirely completely
resurgence energy

salute and replied, "Mr. Ross, Strength Through Discipline, Strength Through Community."

"Very good," Ben said. "Peter, Amy, and Eric, salute and recite our motto with Robert."

The four students obediently saluted and chanted, "Strength Through Discipline, Strength Through Community."

"Brian, Andrea, and Laurie," Mr. Ross commanded. "Join them and repeat."

Now seven students joined in the chant, then fourteen, then twenty, until the whole class was saluting and chanting loudly **in unison**. "Strength Through Discipline, Strength Through Community." Like **a regiment**, Ben thought, just like a regiment.

In the gym after school, David and Eric sat on the floor in their football practice **jerseys**. They were a little early for practice and were having **a heated debate**.

"I think it's dumb," Eric said as he tied the laces on his cleats. "It's just a game in history class, that's all."

"But that doesn't mean it couldn't work." David insisted. "What do you think we learned it for, anyway? To keep it a

....

in unison together; at the same time
a regiment soldiers
jerseys uniforms
a heated debate an argument

secret? I'm telling you, Eric, this is just what the team needs."

"Well, you're gonna have to convince Coach Schiller of that," Eric said. "And I'm not going to tell him."

"What are you scared of?" David asked. "You think Mr. Ross is gonna punish me because I tell a couple of people about The Wave?"

Eric shrugged. "No, man. I think they're gonna laugh."

Brian came out of the locker room and joined them on the floor.

"Hey," David said, "what do you think of us trying to get the rest of the team into The Wave?"

Brian tugged at **his shoulder pads** and thought about it. "You think The Wave could stop that two-hundred-and-twenty-pound linebacker from Clarkstown?" he asked. "I swear, that's all I think about. I keep picturing me calling for the **snap** and then this thing appears in front of me, this giant thing in a Clarkstown uniform. It **steps on my center, it squashes my guards**. It's so big I can't go left, I can't go right, I can't throw over it. . . ." Brian rolled on his back on the floor and pretended someone was bearing down on him. "It just keeps coming and coming. Ahhhhhhhhhh!"

Eric and David laughed, and Brian sat up. "I'll do

----

his shoulder pads part of his uniform

snap ball

steps on my center, it squashes my guards easily tackles the players in front of me so it can tackle me

anything," he told them. "Eat my Wheaties, join The Wave, do my homework. Anything to stop that guy."

More players had gathered around them, including a junior named Deutsch, who was the second-string quarterback behind Brian. Everyone on the team knew that Deutsch wanted nothing more in the world than to **steal Brian's position from him**. As a result, the two of them didn't get along.

"I hear you say you're afraid of the Clarkstown team?" Deutsch asked Brian. "I'll take your place, man, just say the word."

"They let you into the game and we'll **have no chance at all**," Brian told him.

Deutsch sneered. "The only reason you're first string is 'cause you're a senior," he said.

Still sitting on the gym floor, Brian gazed up at the junior. "Man, you **are the most conceited bag of no talent I've ever seen**," he said.

"Oh yeah, look who's talking," Deutsch snarled back.

The next thing David knew, Brian had jumped to his feet and had his fists up. David lunged between the two quarterbacks. "That's just what I was talking about!" he

....

steal Brian's position from him play quarterback

have no chance at all never win

are the most conceited bag of no talent I've ever seen think you are such great player, but you are not

yelled as he pushed them apart. "We're supposed to be a team. We're supposed to support each other. The reason we've been so bad is because all we've been doing is fighting with each other."

More football players were in the gym now. "What's he talking about?" one of them asked.

David turned. "I'm talking about unity. I'm talking about discipline. We have to start acting like a team. Like we have **a common goal**. Your job on this team isn't to steal another guy's position. Your job is to help this team win."

"I could help this team win," Deutsch said. "All Coach Schiller's got to do is make me the first-string quarterback."

"No, man!" David yelled at him. "A bunch of **self-serving individuals** don't make a team. You know why we've done so bad this year? Because we're twenty-five one-man teams all wearing the same Gordon High uniforms. You want to be first-string quarterback on a team that doesn't win? Or do you want to be second-string on a team that does win?"

Deutsch shrugged.

"I'm tired of losing," said another player.

"Yeah," said someone else. "It's **a drag**. This school

....

a common goal the same reason for playing

self-serving individuals people who only care about themselves

a drag not fun

doesn't even take us seriously anymore."

"I'd give up my position and be **a waterboy** if it meant winning a game," said a third.

"Well, we could win," said David. "I'm not saying we'll be able to go out and **destroy** Clarkstown on Saturday, but if we start trying to be a team, I bet we could win a few games this year."

Most of the members of the football team were there by this time, and as David looked around at their faces he could see that they were interested.

"Okay," said one. "What do we do?"

David hesitated for a moment. What they could do was The Wave. But who was he to tell them? He'd only learned of it the day before himself. Suddenly he felt someone nudging him.

"Tell them," Eric whispered. "Tell 'em about The Wave."

What the hell, David thought. "Okay, all I know is you gotta start by learning the mottos. And this is the salute. . . ."

....

a waterboy the boy who serves the team water
destroy beat, defeat
What the hell Why not

CHAPTER 7

That evening Laurie Saunders told her parents about her last two days of history class. The Saunders family was sitting at the dining room table finishing dinner. Through most of the meal, Laurie's father had given them a **stroke-by-stroke** description of the 78 he'd shot in golf that afternoon. Mr. Saunders ran a division of a large **semiconductor company**. Laurie's mother said that she didn't mind his passion for golf because on the course he **managed to get out** all the pressures and frustrations of his job. She said she couldn't explain how he did it, but as long as he came home in a good mood, she wasn't going to argue.

Neither was Laurie, although listening to her father talk about his golf game sometimes bored her to death. It was

....

stroke-by-stroke detailed

semiconductor company business that makes parts for electrical equipment

managed to get out was able to forget

better that he was **easy-going, rather than a worry-wart** like her mother, who was probably the brightest and most perceptive woman Laurie had ever encountered. She practically ran the county's League of Women Voters by herself and was so **politically astute that aspiring politicians seeking** local offices were always asking her to advise them.

For Laurie, her mother was lots of fun when things were going well. She was full of ideas, and you could talk to her for hours. But other times, when Laurie was upset about something or was having a problem, her mother was **murder**—there was no way to hide anything from her. And once Laurie had admitted what the difficulty was, she wouldn't leave her alone.

When Laurie started telling them about The Wave at dinner, it was mostly because she couldn't stand listening to her father talk about golf for another minute. She could tell her mother was bored too. For the last quarter hour Mrs. Saunders had been scratching a wax stain out of the tablecloth with her fingernail.

"It was incredible," Laurie was saying about the class. "Everyone was saluting and repeating the motto. You

....

easy-going, rather than a worry-wart relaxed rather than worried all the time

politically astute that aspiring politicians seeking smart about politics that people who wanted to get elected to

murder difficult to talk to and deal with

couldn't help but get caught up in it. You know, really wanting to make it work. Feeling all that energy building around you."

Mrs. Saunders stopped scratching the tablecloth and looked at her daughter. "I don't think I like it, Laurie. It sounds **too militaristic** to me."

"Oh, Mom," Laurie said, "you always **take things the wrong way**. It's nothing like that. Honest, you'd just have to be there feeling the positive energy in the class to really get what's going on."

Mr. Saunders agreed. "To tell you the truth, I'm for whatever will make these kids pay attention to anything these days."

"And that's what it's really doing, Mom," Laurie said. "Even the bad kids are into it. You know Robert Billings, the class creep? Even he's part of a group. No one's picked on him for two whole days. Tell me that isn't positive."

"But you're supposed to be learning history," Mrs. Saunders argued. "Not how to be part of a group."

"Well, you know," her husband said, "this country was built by people who were part of a group—**the Pilgrims, the Founding Fathers**. I don't think it's wrong for Laurie

....

too militaristic like the army

take things the wrong way misunderstand things

the Pilgrims, the Founding Fathers the early American settlers, the leaders who wrote the United States Constitution

to be learning how to cooperate. If I could get some more cooperation down at the plant instead of this constant **back-biting and bickering** and everyone trying to **cover his own you-know-what**, we wouldn't be behind in production this year."

"I didn't say that it was wrong to cooperate," Mrs. Saunders replied. "But still, people have to do things in their own way. You talk about the greatness of this country and you're talking about people who weren't afraid to act as individuals."

"Mom, I really think you're taking this the wrong way," Laurie said. "Mr. Ross has just found a way to get everybody involved. And we're still doing our homework. It's not like we've forgotten about history."

But her mother was not **to be appeased**. "That's all very well and good. But it just doesn't sound like the right thing for you, Laurie. Babe, we've raised you to be an individual."

Laurie's father turned to his wife. "Midge, don't you think you're taking all this a little too seriously? A little bit of community spirit is a terrific thing for these kids."

"That's right, Mom," Laurie said, smiling. "Haven't you

....

back-biting and bickering complaining and fighting

cover his own you-know-what blame other people for problems

to be appeased going to stop talking about it

always said that I was a little too independent?"

Mrs. Saunders was not amused. "Honey, just remember that the popular thing is not always the right thing."

"Oh, Mom," Laurie said, annoyed that her mother would not **see her side of the argument** at all. "Either you're being stubborn or you just don't understand this at all."

"Really, Midge," Mr. Saunders said. "I'm sure Laurie's history teacher knows exactly what he's doing. I don't see why you should make this into a big deal."

"You don't think it's dangerous to allow a teacher to **manipulate** students like that?" Mrs. Saunders asked her husband.

"Mr. Ross isn't manipulating us," Laurie said. "He's one of my best teachers. He knows what he's doing, and as far as I'm concerned what he's doing is for the class's good. I wish some of my other teachers were as interesting."

Laurie's mother seemed ready to keep arguing, but her husband changed the subject. "Where's David tonight?" he asked. "Isn't he coming over?" David often came over in the evening, usually **on the pretense of studying** with Laurie. But inevitably he'd wind up in the den with Mr. Saunders talking about sports or engineering. Since David hoped to

....

see her side of the argument listen to her

manipulate influence and try to control

on the pretense of studying with the excuse that he wanted to study

study engineering just as Mr. Saunders had, they had lots to talk about. Mr. Saunders had also played high school football. Mrs. Saunders had once told Laurie that it was **surely a match made in heaven**.

Laurie shook her head. "He's home studying tomorrow's history assignment."

Mr. Saunders looked surprised. "David studying? Now *there's* something to be concerned about."

Because Ben and Christy Ross both taught full time at the high school, they had grown accustomed to sharing many of the after-school chores around their house—cooking, cleaning, and running errands. That afternoon Christy had to take her car into the shop to get the muffler replaced, so Ben had agreed that he'd cook. But after that history class he **felt too preoccupied** to bother cooking. Instead he stopped at the Chinese **take-out place** on the way home and picked up some eggrolls and egg foo yung.

When Christy got home around dinnertime, she found the table not covered with plates for dinner, but with books, again. Looking over the brown paper take-out bags on the kitchen counter, she asked, "You call this dinner?"

....

surely a match made in heaven a relationship that was meant to be; a good relationship that would last

felt too preoccupied was too busy thinking

take-out place restaurant

Ben looked up from the table. "I'm sorry, Chris. I'm just so preoccupied with this class. And I've got so much to do to prepare for it, I didn't want to take time to cook."

Christy nodded. It wasn't as if he did this every time it was his turn to cook. She could forgive him this time. She started unpacking the food. "So how is your experiment going, Dr. Frankenstein? Have your monsters turned on you yet?"

"**On the contrary**," her husband replied. "Most of them are actually turning into human beings!"

"You don't say," said Christy.

"I happen to know that they're all **keeping up on their reading**," Ben said. "Some of them are even reading ahead. It's as if they suddenly love being **prepared for class**."

"Or they're suddenly afraid of being unprepared," his wife observed.

But Ben ignored her comment. "No, I really think they've improved. At least, they're behaving better."

Christy shook her head. "These can't be the same kids I have for music."

"I'm telling you," her husband said, "it's amazing how much more they like you when you make decisions for them."

....

On the contrary Just the opposite
keeping up on their reading doing their homework
prepared for class ready to answer questions and take notes

"Sure, it means less work for *them*. They don't have to think for themselves," Christy said. "But now stop reading and clear some of those books away so we can eat."

As Ben made room on the kitchen table, Christy set the food out. When Ben stood up Christy thought he was going to help her, but instead he started pacing around the kitchen, deep in thought. Christy went on getting the meal ready, but she too was thinking about The Wave. There was something about it that bothered her, something about the **tone** of her husband's voice when he spoke about his class—as if they were now better students than the rest of the school. As she sat down at the table she said, "How **far do you plan to push this**, Ben?"

"I don't know," Ross answered. "But I think it could be fascinating to see."

Christy watched her husband pace around the kitchen, lost in thought. "Why don't you sit down?" she said. "Your egg foo yung's going to get cold."

"You know," her husband said as he came to the table and sat down, "the funny thing is, I feel myself getting caught up in it, too. It's contagious."

Christy nodded. That was obvious. "Maybe you're

....

tone sound

far do you plan to push this long are you going to keep doing this experiment

becoming **a guinea pig** in your own experiment," she said. Although she made it sound like a joke, she was hoping he'd take it as a warning.

....

a guinea pig the one who is being tested

BEFORE YOU MOVE ON...

1. **Simile** On page 67, Mr. Ross thinks the class acts "like a regiment." What does this mean?

2. **Character's Motive** On page 71, David begins to teach his football team The Wave's motto. Why?

LOOK AHEAD Read pages 81–106 to see how The Wave changes the school.

CHAPTER 8

Both David and Laurie lived within walking distance of Gordon High. David's route didn't necessarily lead past Laurie's house, but ever since tenth grade he'd always **gone out of his way**. When he first noticed her, as a sophomore, he used to walk down her street on the way to school every morning, hoping that he would pass her house just as she was leaving for school. At first he managed to **run into her** only about once a week. But as the weeks passed and they got to know each other, he began to catch her more frequently until, by the spring, they walked together almost every day. For a long time David thought this was just a matter of luck and good timing. **It never occurred to him** that from the beginning Laurie had waited at her window,

....

gone out of his way walked to Laurie's house first
run into her see her
It never occurred to him He never thought

watching for him. At first she had only pretended to "run into" him once a week. Later she "ran into" him more often.

When David picked Laurie up to walk with her to school the next morning, he was **bursting with brainstorms**. "I'm telling you, Laurie," he said as they walked along a sidewalk toward school. "This is just what the football team needs."

"What the football team needs," Laurie told him, "is a quarterback who can pass, a running back who doesn't **fumble**, a couple of linebackers who aren't afraid to tackle, an end who—"

"Stop it," David said irritably. "I'm serious. I got the team into it yesterday. Brian and Eric helped me. The guys really **responded to** it. I mean, it's not like we improved in only one practice, but I could feel it. I could really feel the team spirit. Even Coach Schiller was impressed. He said we were like a new team."

"My mother says it sounds like **brainwashing to her**," Laurie said.

"What?"

"She says Mr. Ross is manipulating us."

"She's crazy," David said. "How could she know? And

....

bursting with brainstorms full of ideas
fumble drop the ball
responded to liked, accepted
brainwashing to her we are being told what to think

besides, what do you care what your mother says? You know she worries about everything."

"I didn't say I agreed with her," Laurie said.

"Well, you didn't say you disagreed with her either," David said.

"I was just telling you what she said," Laurie replied.

David **wouldn't let it drop**. "How does she know, anyway? She can't possibly understand what The Wave is about unless she's been in class to see it work. Parents always think they know everything!"

Laurie suddenly felt an urge to disagree with him, but she restrained herself. She didn't want to start a fight with David over something so petty. She hated it when they **quarreled**. Besides, for all she knew, The Wave might be just what the football team needed. They certainly needed *something*. She decided to change the subject. "Did you find help for calculus?"

David shrugged. "Naw, the only kids who know anything are in my class."

"So why not ask one of them?"

"No way," David said. "I don't want any of them to know **I'm having trouble**."

....

wouldn't let it drop continued to talk about it
quarreled argued
I'm having trouble I do not understand the math problems

"Why not?" Laurie asked. "I'm sure someone would help you."

"Of course they would," David said. "But I don't want their help."

Laurie sighed. It was true that lots of kids at school were competitive about grades and **class standing**. But few took it as far as David did. "Well," she said, "I know Amy didn't say anything at lunch, but if you can't find anyone else she could probably help you."

"Amy?"

"She's incredibly smart in math," Laurie explained. "I bet you could give her your problem and she'd **have it figured out** in ten minutes."

"But I asked her at lunch," David said.

"She was just being shy," Laurie said. "I think she likes Brian and she just doesn't want to **intimidate him by seeming too brainy**."

David laughed. "I don't think she has to worry, Laurie. The only way she could intimidate him was if she weighed two hundred pounds and wore a Clarkstown uniform."

When the students arrived in class that day, there was

....

class standing which students were the smartest
have it figured out solve it
intimidate him by seeming too brainy scare him by acting too smart

a large poster in the back of the room with a blue wave symbol on it. They found Mr. Ross dressed differently than usual. Where before he'd come to class in casual clothes, today he wore a blue suit, white shirt, and a tie. The students went quickly to their seats as their teacher walked up and down the aisles passing out small yellow cards.

Brad nudged Laurie. "It's not time for report cards," he whispered.

Laurie stared at the card she'd received. "It's a Wave **membership card**," she whispered back.

"What?" Brad hissed.

"All right," Mr. Ross slapped his hands together loudly. "No talking."

Brad sat up straight in his seat. But Laurie understood his surprise. Membership cards? It must have been a joke. Meanwhile, Mr. Ross had finished **distributing** the cards and stood in the front of the room.

"Now you will all have membership cards," Mr. Ross announced. "If you turn them over you will find that some of them have been marked with a red X. If you have a red X you are to be a monitor, and you will report directly to me any members of The Wave who do not obey our rules."

....

membership card card that proves students are members of The Wave

distributing passing out

Around the room students were **scrutinizing** their cards and turning them over to see if they had a red X. Those who had them, like Robert and Brian, were smiling. Those who didn't, like Laurie, seemed less pleased.

Laurie raised her hand.

"Yes, Laurie," Ben said.

"Uh, **what's the point of this**?" Laurie asked.

There was a silence around the room and Ben did not answer right away. Then he said, "Aren't you forgetting something?"

"Oh, right." Laurie got up and stood next to her desk. "Mr. Ross, what's the point of these cards?"

Ben had expected someone to question him on the cards. The reason for them would not be **apparent** immediately. For now he said, "It's just an example of how a group might **monitor itself**."

Laurie had no other questions, so Ben turned to the blackboard and added another word to "Strength Through Discipline, Strength Through Community." Today's word was "Action."

"Now that we understand Discipline and Community," he told the class, "Action is our next lesson. Ultimately,

....

scrutinizing examining; closely looking at
what's the point of this why did you give us these cards
apparent clear
monitor itself watch over its members; control its members

discipline and community are meaningless without action. Discipline gives you the right to action. A disciplined group with a goal can take action to achieve it. They *must* take action to achieve it. Class, do you believe in The Wave?"

There was a split-second hesitation, and then the class rose in unison and answered in what seemed like a single voice. "Mr. Ross, yes!"

Mr. Ross nodded. "Then you must take action! Never be afraid to act on what you believe. As The Wave you must act together like a well-oiled machine. Through hard work and **allegiance** to each other, you will learn faster and accomplish more. But only if you support one another, and only if you work together and obey the rules, can you ensure the success of The Wave."

As he spoke, the class members stood beside their desks at attention. Laurie Saunders stood with them, but she did not feel the high energy and unity she'd felt on previous days. In fact, today there was something about the class, something about **their single mindedness and absolute obedience to** Mr. Ross that she would almost describe as **creepy**.

"Be seated," Mr. Ross ordered, and instantly the class sat. Their teacher continued his lesson. "When we first began

....

allegiance loyalty

their single mindedness and absolute obedience to the way they were all acting the same and not questioning

creepy a little frightening

The Wave a few days ago I felt that some of you were actually competing to give the right answers and to be better members than others. From now on I want this to end. You are not competing against each other, you are working together **for a common cause**. You must conceive of yourselves as a team, a team of which you are all members. Remember, in The Wave you are all equals. No one is more important or more popular than anyone else and no one is to be excluded from the group. Community means equality within the group.

"Now your first action as a team will be to actively recruit new members. To become a member of The Wave, each new student must demonstrate knowledge of our rules and **pledge strict obedience to** them."

David smiled as Eric looked over at him and winked. This was what he'd needed to hear. There was nothing wrong with **turning other kids on to** The Wave. It was for the good of everybody. Especially the football team.

Mr. Ross had concluded his talk on The Wave. He intended to spend the rest of the period reviewing the assignment he'd given the class the night before. But suddenly a student named George Snyder was raising his hand.

....

for a common cause to reach the same goal
pledge strict obedience to promise to always obey
turning other kids on to getting other students to join

"Yes, George."

George sprang from his seat to attention by his desk. "Mr. Ross, for the first time I feel like I'm part of something," he announced. "Something great."

Around the room, **startled** students stared at George. Feeling the eyes of the class upon him, George began to sink back into his chair. But then Robert suddenly stood.

"Mr. Ross," he said proudly, "I know just how George feels. It's like **being born again**."

No sooner had he returned to his seat than Amy stood. "George's right, Mr. Ross. I feel the same way."

David was pleased. He knew that what George had done was **corny**, but then Robert and Amy had done it, too, just so George wouldn't feel foolish and alone. That's what was good about The Wave. They supported each other. Now he stood up and said, "Mr. Ross, I'm proud of The Wave."

This sudden outburst of testimonials surprised Ben. He was determined to get on to the day's classwork, but suddenly he knew he had to go along with the class a little longer. Almost **subconsciously** he sensed how much they wanted him to lead them, and it was something he felt he could not deny.

....

startled surprised
being born again starting all over
corny silly
subconsciously without thinking

"Our salute!" he ordered. Around the room students jumped to attention beside their desks and gave The Wave salute. The mottos followed: "Strength Through Discipline, Strength Through Community, Strength Through Action!"

Mr. Ross was picking up his class notes when the students burst forth again, this time giving the salute and chanting their motto without **prompting**. Then silence fell over the room. Mr. Ross gazed at the students in **wonderment**. The Wave was no longer just an idea or a game. It was a **living movement in** his students. They *were* The Wave now, and Ben realized that they could act on their own without him if they wanted. That thought could have been frightening, but Ben was confident that he had control as their leader. The experiment was simply becoming much more interesting.

At lunch that day all The Wave members who were in the cafeteria sat at a single long table. Brian, Brad, Amy, Laurie, and David were there. At first Robert Billings seemed **tentative** about joining them, but when David saw him he insisted he sit at the table, telling him they were all part of The Wave now.

....

prompting being asked
wonderment amazement
living movement in real thing to
tentative shy, hesitant

Most of the kids were **raving** about what was going on in Mr. Ross's class, and Laurie really had no reason to argue with them. But still she felt odd—all that saluting and chanting. Finally, during a pause in the conversation, she said, "Does anyone feel kind of strange about this?"

David turned to her. "What do you mean?"

"I don't know," Laurie said. "But doesn't it feel a little weird?"

"It's just so different," Amy told her. "That's why it feels weird."

"Yeah," Brad said. "It's like there's no **in-crowd** anymore. Man, the thing that bugs me the most about school sometimes is all these little **cliques**. I'm tired of feeling like every day's a big popularity contest. That's what's so great about The Wave. You don't have to worry about how popular you are. We're all equal. We're all part of the same community."

"Do you think everyone likes that?" Laurie asked.

"Do you know anyone who doesn't?" David asked.

Laurie felt **her face grow flushed**. "Well, I'm not sure I do."

Suddenly Brian pulled something out of his pocket and held it up to Laurie. "Hey, don't forget," he said. He was

....

raving talking excitedly
in-crowd popular group
cliques groups of people who exclude others
her face grow flushed herself become embarrassed

holding up his Wave membership card with the red *X* on the back.

"Forget what?" Laurie asked.

"You know," Brian said. "What Mr. Ross said about reporting anyone who breaks the rules."

Laurie was shocked. Brian really couldn't be serious, could he? Now Brian started to grin, and she relaxed.

"Besides," David said. "Laurie isn't breaking any rule."

"If she was really against The Wave she would be," Robert said.

The rest of the table became silent, surprised that Robert had said anything. Some of them weren't even used to hearing his voice, he usually **said so little**.

"What I mean is," Robert said nervously, "the whole idea of The Wave is that the people in it have to support it. If we're really a community, we all have to agree."

Laurie was about to say something, but she stopped herself. It was The Wave that had given Robert the courage to sit at the table with them and to join in the conversation. If she argued against The Wave now, she would really be **implying that** Robert should go sit by himself again and not be part of their "community."

....

said so little didn't talk
implying that making it seem as if she thought

Brad patted Robert on his back. "Hey, I'm glad you joined us," he said.

Robert blushed and then turned to David. "Did he stick anything on my back?" he asked. Everyone at the table laughed.

CHAPTER 9

Ben Ross **wasn't quite sure what to make of** The Wave. What had begun as a simple history experiment had become a fad that was spreading outside his classroom. As a result, some unexpected things had started to occur. For one, the size of his daily history class was beginning to expand as students from free periods, study halls, and lunch came to be part of The Wave. The recruiting of more students for The Wave had apparently been far more successful than he had ever expected. So successful, in fact, that Ben began to **suspect** that some students were **cutting** other classes to sit in on his.

Remarkably enough, though, even with the larger class size and the students' insistence on practicing the salute and

....

wasn't quite sure what to make of did not know what to think about

suspect think, believe

cutting not going to; skipping

motto, the class was not falling behind. If anything, they were covering their assigned lessons even faster than usual. Using the rapid question and answer style that The Wave had inspired, they had quickly covered Japan's entrance into World War Two. Ben noticed a marked improvement in preparation for class and in class participation, but he also noticed that there was less thinking behind the preparation. His students could **glibly spit back** answers as if **by rote**, but there was **no analysis**, no questioning on their part. In a way he could not fault them, because he himself had introduced them to the ways of The Wave. It was just another unexpected development in the experiment.

Ben reasoned that the students realized that to neglect their studies would **be detrimental to** The Wave. The only way they could have time to spend on The Wave was to be so well prepared that they only needed half the regular class to cover their assigned lessons. But he wasn't certain this was something to be pleased about. The class's homework assignments had improved, but rather than long, thoughtful answers, they wrote short ones. On a multiple choice test they might all do well, but Ben had his doubts about how they'd do on an exam consisting of essays.

....

glibly spit back quickly give
by rote they had memorized them
no analysis no thinking about the answers
be detrimental to hurt

To add to the interesting developments in his experiment was a report he'd heard that David Collins and his friends Eric and Brian had successfully infused The Wave into the school's football team. Over the years, Norm Schiller, the biology teacher who also coached the school's football team, had become so **soured by wisecracks** about the team's continual losses that during football season he practically went months without speaking to another teacher. But that morning in the faculty lounge Norm had actually thanked him for introducing The Wave to his students. **Would wonders never cease?**

On his own, Ben had tried to find out what it was that attracted students to The Wave. Some of those he asked said it was just something new and different, like any fad. Others said they liked the democracy of it—the fact that they were all equals now. It pleased Ross to hear that answer. He enjoyed thinking that he had helped **break down the petty** popularity contests and cliques that he felt often preoccupied too much of his students' thinking and energy. A few students even said they thought the idea of increased discipline was good for them. That had surprised Ben. Over the years, discipline had become an increasingly personal

....

soured by wisecracks bitter because of discouraging comments

Would wonders never cease? What other unbelievable events would happen?

break down the petty get rid of the school's silly

responsibility. If the students didn't do it themselves, their teachers **were less and less inclined to step in**. Maybe this was a mistake, Ben thought. Perhaps one of the results of his experiment would be a general rebirth of school discipline. He even daydreamed about a story in the education section of *Time* magazine: *Discipline Returns to the Classroom: Teacher Makes Startling Discovery.*

Laurie Saunders sat on a desk in the school publications office, chewing on the end of a pen. Various members of *The Gordon Grapevine* staff sat on desks around her, biting their nails or chewing gum. Alex Cooper was **wearing his Sony radio** and was bopping to the music through his earphones. Another reporter was wearing roller skates. This was *The Grapevine's* excuse for a weekly **editorial meeting**.

"Okay," Laurie told them. "We've got the same problem as usual. The paper is due out next week, but we don't have enough stories." Laurie looked at the girl wearing roller skates. "Jeanie, you were supposed to do a fashion story on the latest clothes. Where is it?"

"Oh, nobody's wearing anything interesting this year," Jeanie replied. "It's always the same thing: jeans and sneakers

....

were less and less inclined to step in did not feel it was their job to discipline their students

wearing his Sony radio listening to a small radio

editorial meeting meeting about the stories for the next issue of the paper

and T-shirts."

"Well then write about how there are no new styles this year," Laurie said, then she turned to the reporter who was bopping to his radio. "Alex?"

Alex kept bopping. He couldn't hear her.

"Alex!" Laurie said more loudly.

Finally someone near Alex gave him a nudge. He looked up, startled. "Uh, yeah?"

Laurie **rolled her eyes**. "Alex, this is supposed to be an editorial meeting."

"Really?" Alex replied.

"Okay, so where's your record review for this issue?" Laurie asked.

"Oh, uh, yeah, record review, right, uh, yeah," Alex said. "Well, uh, you see, it's a long story. Uh, like I was going to do it but, uh, remember that trip I said I had to take to Argentina?"

Laurie rolled her eyes again.

"Well, it **fell through**," Alex said. "And I had to go to Hong Kong instead."

Laurie turned to Alex's sidekick, Carl. "I suppose you had to go to Hong Kong with him," she said sarcastically.

....

rolled her eyes made a face to show she was upset
fell through did not happen

Carl shook his head. "No," he replied seriously, "I made the trip to Argentina as scheduled."

"I see," said Laurie. She looked around at the rest of *The Grapevine's* staff. "I suppose the rest of you have been too busy **hopping around the globe** to get anything written as well."

"I went to the movies," Jeanie said.

"Did you write a review?" Laurie asked.

"No, it was too good," she replied.

"Too good?"

"It's no fun writing reviews of good movies," she said.

"Yeah," said Alex, the globe-hopping record reviewer. "It's no fun doing a review of a good movie because you can't say anything bad about it. The only time it's fun to review something is when it's bad. Then you can **tear it to shreds**, he, he, he." Alex started rubbing his hands together as he **went into his mad scientist routine**. Alex had the best mad scientist routine in school. He also did a great imitation of a wind surfer in a hurricane.

"We need stories for the paper," Laurie said resolutely. "Doesn't anyone have any ideas?"

"They got a new school bus," someone said.

....

hopping around the globe traveling the world

tear it to shreds criticize it

went into his mad scientist routine pretended to be a crazy scientist

"Whoopee!"

"I heard that Mr. Gabondi's **going on sabbatical** next year."

"Maybe he won't come back."

"Some kid in the tenth grade put his fist through a window yesterday. He was trying to prove that you could punch a hole in a window and not cut yourself."

"Did he do it?"

"Nope, got twelve stitches."

"Hey, wait a minute," said Carl. "What about this Wave thing? Everyone wants to know what it is."

"Aren't you in Ross's history class, Laurie?" another staff member asked.

"That's probably the biggest story in school right now," said a third.

Laurie nodded. She was aware that The Wave was worth a story, and maybe a big story at that. A couple of days ago it had even occurred to her that something like The Wave was probably just what the **sluggish**, disorganized staff of *The Grapevine* itself needed. But she had **set the idea aside**. She couldn't even explain her decision **consciously**. It was just that creepy feeling she'd begun to get, the feeling that

....

going on sabbatical not going to teach

sluggish lazy

set the idea aside decided it was not a good idea

consciously in words

maybe they should be careful with The Wave. So far she'd seen it do some good in Mr. Ross's class and David said he thought it was helping the football team. But still she was **cautious**.

"Well, **what about it**, Laurie?" someone asked.

"The Wave?" Laurie said.

"How come you haven't assigned that story to us?" Alex asked. "Or are you just saving the good ones for yourself?"

"I don't know if anyone knows enough about it to write about it yet," Laurie said.

"What do you mean? You're in The Wave, aren't you?" Alex asked.

"Well, yes I am," Laurie replied. "But I still . . . I still don't know."

A couple of the staff members scowled. "Well, I think *The Grapevine* still should have a story reporting that it exists, at least," Carl said. "I mean, a lot of kids are wondering what it is."

Laurie nodded. "Okay, you're right. I'll try to explain what it is. But **in the meantime**, I want you all to do something. Since we still have a few days before the paper has to come out. Try to find out everything you can about

....

cautious careful

what about it what do you know about it

in the meantime while I am doing that

what kids think of The Wave."

Ever since the night she had first discussed The Wave with her mother and father at dinner, Laurie had purposely avoided the subject at home. It didn't seem worth creating any more **hassles**, especially with her mother, who could find something to worry about in everything Laurie did, whether it was going out late with David, chewing on a pen, or The Wave. Laurie just hoped her mother would forget about it. But that night while she was studying in her room her mother knocked on the door. "Babe, can I come in?"

"Sure, Mom."

The door opened and Mrs. Saunders stepped in, wearing a yellow terrycloth bathrobe and slippers. The skin around her eyes looked greasy, and Laurie knew she'd been putting wrinkle cream on.

"How're the **crow's feet**, Mom?" she asked in good-natured humor.

Mrs. Saunders smiled wryly at her daughter. "Someday," she said, **wagging a finger**, "someday you won't think it's so funny." She walked over to the desk and **peered** over her daughter's shoulders at the book she was reading.

....

hassles trouble
crow's feet wrinkles around your eyes
wagging a finger pointing at Laurie
peered looked

"Shakespeare?"

"What'd you expect?" Laurie asked.

"Well, anything except The Wave," Mrs. Saunders said, sitting down on her daughter's bed.

Laurie turned to look at her. "What do you mean, Mom?"

"Only that I met Elaine Billings at the supermarket today, and she told me Robert is **a completely new person**."

"Was she worried?" Laurie asked.

"No, she wasn't, but I am," Mrs. Saunders said. "You know, they've been having problems with him for years. Elaine has talked to me frequently about it. She's been very worried."

Laurie nodded.

"So she's ecstatic about this sudden change," Mrs. Saunders said. "But somehow I don't trust it. **Such a dramatic personality change.** It almost sounds like he's joined a **cult** or something."

"What do you mean?"

"Laurie, if you study the types of people who join these cults, they're almost always people who are unhappy with themselves and their lives. They look at the cult as a way

....

a completely new person acting differently

Such a dramatic personality change. He has completely changed how he behaves.

cult group that takes control over its members

of changing, of starting over, of literally being born again. How else do you explain the change in Robert?"

"But what's wrong with that, Mom?"

"The problem is that it's not real, Laurie. Robert is safe only as long as he **keeps within the confines** of The Wave. But what do you think happens when he leaves it? The outside world doesn't know or care about The Wave. If Robert **couldn't function** in school before The Wave, he won't be able to function outside of school where The Wave doesn't exist."

Laurie understood. "Well, you don't have to worry about me, Mom. I don't think I'm as **crazy about it** as I was a couple of days ago."

Mrs. Saunders nodded. "No, I didn't think you would be, once you thought about it for a while."

"So what's the problem?" Laurie asked.

"The problem is everyone else at school who still takes it seriously," her mother said.

"Oh, Mom, you're the one who's taking this too seriously. Do you want to know what I think? I think it's just a fad. It's like **punk rock** or something. In two months no one will even remember what The Wave was."

....

keeps within the confines is with other members
couldn't function was not able to act normally
crazy about it supportive; interested in it
punk rock a new kind of music

"Mrs. Billings told me that they're organizing a Wave rally for Friday afternoon," Mrs. Saunders said.

"It's just **a pep rally** for the football game on Saturday," Laurie explained. "The only difference is they're calling it a Wave rally instead of a pep rally."

"At which they will formally **indoctrinate** two hundred new members?" Mrs. Saunders asked skeptically.

Laurie sighed. "Mom, listen to me. You're really getting paranoid about this whole thing. Nobody's indoctrinating anyone. They're going to welcome new members to The Wave at the rally. Those people would have come to the pep rally anyway. Really, Mom, The Wave is just a game. It's like little boys playing soldier. I wish you could meet Mr. Ross because then you'd see there's nothing to worry about. He's such a good teacher. He'd never get into anything like cults."

"And you're not disturbed by it at all?" Mrs. Saunders asked.

"Mom, the only thing that disturbs me is that so many kids in my class could allow themselves to get caught up in something so immature. I mean, I guess I can understand why David is into it. He's convinced that it's going to

---

a pep rally an assembly to show support
indoctrinate add and instruct

turn the football team into a winner. But it's Amy I can't understand. I mean, well, you know Amy. She's so bright and yet, I see her taking this so seriously."

"So you *are* worried," her mother said.

But Laurie shook her head. "No, Mom. That's the only thing that bothers me, and that isn't much. I promise you, Mom, **this is a molehill and you're looking for a mountain**. Really, trust me."

Mrs. Saunders rose slowly. "Well, all right, Laurie. At least I know you're not involved in this situation. I suppose that's enough to be thankful for. But please, babe, be careful." She leaned over, kissed her daughter on the forehead, and left the room.

For a few minutes Laurie sat at her desk but did not go back to her homework. Instead, she chewed on a Bic pen and thought about her mother's concerns. She really was **blowing it way out of proportion**, wasn't she? It really was just a fad, wasn't it?

....

this is a molehill and you're looking for a mountain this is not as big of a problem as you think it is

blowing it way out of proportion getting worried for no reason

BEFORE YOU MOVE ON...

1. **Predict** Many students think The Wave works. How might their new beliefs affect their future behavior?

2. **Inference** Laurie does not believe in The Wave. Why doesn't she speak out against it?

LOOK AHEAD Read pages 107–120 to see what is in the letter Laurie receives.

CHAPTER 10

Ben Ross was having coffee in the faculty lounge when someone came in and told him Principal Owens wanted to see him in his office. Ross felt a **tremor of nervousness**. Had something **gone wrong**? If Owens wanted to see him, it had to be about The Wave.

Ross stepped out into the hall and started down toward the principal's office. On the way more than a dozen students paused to give him The Wave salute. He returned them and continued quickly, wondering what Owens was going to say. In one sense, if Owens was going to tell him that there had been complaints and that he should stop the experiment, Ross knew he would feel some relief. Honestly, he had never expected The Wave to **spread this far**. The

....

tremor of nervousness little nervous
gone wrong bad happened because of The Wave
spread this far become this popular

news that kids in other classes, kids in other grades even, had gotten into The Wave still amazed him. He simply hadn't **intended** it to be anything like this.

And yet there was another **consideration**, the **so-called losers** in the class—Robert Billings, for example. For the first time in his life, Robert was an equal, a member, part of the group. No one was making fun of him anymore, no one was giving him a hard time. And the change in Robert was indeed remarkable. Not only had his appearance improved, but he was starting to **contribute**. For the first time he was an active member of his class. And it wasn't just history. Christy said she was noticing it in music too. Robert seemed like a new person. To end The Wave might mean returning Robert to the role of class creep and taking away the only chance he had.

And wouldn't ending the experiment now also cheat the other students who were taking part in it? Ben wondered. They would be left hanging without a chance to see where it would eventually lead them. And he would lose the chance to lead them there.

Ben abruptly stopped. Hey, wait a minute. Since when was he leading them anywhere? This was a classroom

....

intended planned
consideration thing to think about
so-called losers outcasts
contribute talk in class; share his ideas

experiment, remember? An opportunity for his students to **get a taste** of what life in Nazi Germany might have been like. Ross smiled to himself. Let's not get carried away, he thought, and continued down the hall.

Principal Owens's door was open, and when he saw Ben Ross enter the anteroom, he motioned him in with a wave.

Ben was slightly confused. On the way down to the office he'd somehow convinced himself that Principal Owens was going to **chew him out**, but the old man appeared to be in a good mood.

Principal Owens was a towering man who stood over six feet four inches. His head was almost completely bald except for a few tufts of hair above either ear. His only other noteworthy feature was his pipe, always present, which protruded from his lips. He had a deep voice, and when he was angry he might **instill instant religion in the most hardened atheist**. But today it seemed as if Ben had nothing to fear.

Principal Owens sat behind his desk, his large black shoes propped up on one corner, and squinted slightly at Ben. "Say, Ben, that's a good-looking suit," he said. Owens himself had never been seen around Gordon High in less

---

get a taste experience a little

chew him out yell at him

instill instant religion in the most hardened atheist frighten anyone into agreeing with him

than a three-piece, even at a Saturday football game.

"Thank you, sir," Ben replied nervously.

Principal Owens smiled. "I can't recall seeing you in one before."

"Uh, yes, this is something new for me," Ben allowed.

One of the principal's eyebrows rose. "Wouldn't have anything to do with this Wave thing, would it?"

Ben had to clear his throat. "Well, yes it does, actually."

Principal Owens leaned forward. "Now, tell me, Ben, what this Wave thing is all about," he said. "You've got the **school in a tizzy**."

"Well, I hope it's a good tizzy," Ben Ross replied.

Principal Owens rubbed his chin. "From what I've heard it is. Have you heard differently?"

Ben knew he had to **reassure him**. He quickly shook his head. "No sir, I've heard nothing."

The principal nodded. "**I'm all ears**, Ben."

Ben took a deep breath and began. "It started several days ago in my senior history class. We were watching a film about the Nazis and . . ."

When he finished explaining The Wave, Ben noticed that Principal Owens looked less happy than before, but not

....

school in a tizzy whole school talking about it
reassure him make the principal think everything was fine
I'm all ears Tell me all about it

as noticeably displeased as Ben had feared he might be. The principal removed his pipe from between his lips and tapped it on an ashtray. "I must say it's unusual, Ben. Are you sure that the students are not falling behind?"

"If anything, they're ahead," Ben replied.

"But there are students outside your class that are now involved with this," the principal observed.

"But there have been no complaints," Ben said. "In fact Christy says she's even noticed an improvement in her classes because of it." This was a slight exaggeration, Ben knew. But he also felt it was necessary because Owens **was overreacting to** The Wave.

"Still, Ben, these mottos and this saluting bother me," the principal said.

"It shouldn't," Ben replied. "It's just part of the game. And also, Norm Schiller—"

"Yes, yes, I know," Owens said, cutting him short. "He was in here yesterday raving about this thing. He says it's literally turned that football team of his around. The way he was talking, Ben, you would have thought he'd just drafted six future **Heisman Trophy winners. Frankly,** I'd just like to see them beat Clarkstown on Saturday." The

....

was overreacting to seemed overly worried about
Heisman Trophy winners championship football players
Frankly, Honestly,

principal paused momentarily and then said, "But that's not what I'm concerned about, Ben. I'm concerned about the students. This Wave thing seems too open ended for my liking. I know you haven't broken any rules, but there are limits."

"I'm completely aware of that," Ben insisted. "You have to understand that this experiment can't go any further than I let it go. The whole basis for The Wave is the idea of a group willing to follow their leader. And as long as I'm involved in this, I assure you it can't get **out of hand**."

Principal Owens refilled his pipe with fresh tobacco and lit it, for a moment disappearing behind a small cloud of smoke while he considered Ben's words. "Okay," he said. "To be perfectly frank about this, it's so different from anything we've ever had around here that I'm not sure what to think. I say, let's **keep an eye on** this thing, Ben. And keep your ears open too. Remember, Ben, this experiment, if that's what you want to call it, involves **young, impressionable kids**. Sometimes we forget that they are young and haven't developed the, uh, the judgment we hope they'll someday have. Sometimes they can take something too far if they're not watched. Understand?"

---

out of hand out of control

keep an eye on be watchful of

young, impressionable kids kids who can be easily influenced and do not always think for themselves

"Absolutely."

"You promise me I'm not going to have **a parade of** parents down here suddenly shouting that we're indoctrinating their kids with something?"

"I promise," Ben said.

Principal Owens nodded slightly. "Well, I can't say that **I'm crazy about** this, but you've never **given me cause to doubt you** before."

"And I won't now," Ben told him.

....

a parade of a lot of

I'm crazy about I am completely comfortable with

given me cause to doubt you done anything that would make me not trust you

CHAPTER 11

When Laurie Saunders got to the publications office the next day, she found a plain white envelope on the floor. Early that morning, or late the afternoon before, someone must have **slipped** it under the door. Laurie picked it up and closed the door behind her. Inside the envelope was a handwritten story with a note attached. Laurie read the note:

Dear Editors of *The Grapevine*,

This is a story I have written for *The Grapevine*. Don't bother looking for my name because you won't find it. I don't want my friends or other kids to know I wrote this.

....

slipped put

Scowling, Laurie turned to the story. At the top of the page the **anonymous** author had written a title:

Welcome to the Wave—or Else

I'm a junior here at Gordon High. Three or four days ago me and my friends heard about this thing called The Wave that all the seniors were getting into. We got interested. You know how juniors always want to be like the seniors.

*A **bunch** of us went to Mr. Ross's class to see what it was. Some of my friends liked what we heard, but some of us weren't sure. It looked like a dumb game to me.*

When the class was over, we started to leave. But this senior stopped us in the hall. I didn't know him, but he said he was in Mr. Ross's class and asked did we want to join The Wave. Two of my friends said yes and two said they didn't know and I said I wasn't interested.

This senior started telling us how great The Wave was. He said that the more kids who joined, the better it would get. He said almost all the seniors at school had joined and most of the juniors, too.

....

anonymous unknown
bunch group

*Pretty soon my two friends who said first they didn't know changed their minds and said they wanted to join. Then the senior turned to me. "Aren't you going to **stick** with your friends?" he asked.*

I told him they were still my friends even if I didn't join. He kept asking me why I didn't want to join. I just told him I didn't feel like it.

Then he got mad. He said pretty soon people in The Wave wouldn't want to be friends with people who weren't in it. He even said I'd lose all my friends if I didn't join. I think he was trying to scare me.

*But **it backfired on him**. One of my friends said he didn't see why anyone had to join who didn't want to. My other friends agreed and we left.*

*Today I found out that three of my friends joined after some other seniors talked to them. I saw that senior from Mr. Ross's class in the hall and he asked if I had joined yet. I told him I didn't intend to. He said if I didn't join soon **it would be too late**.*

All I want to know is: Too late for what?

Laurie refolded the story and put it back in the envelope.

....

stick join the group
it backfired on him his plan did not work
it would be too late I would not be able to join later

Her thoughts about The Wave were beginning to **come into focus**.

As Ben left Principal Owens's office he saw several students putting up a large Wave banner in the hall. It was the day of the pep rally—the Wave rally, Ross had to remind himself. There were more students in the halls now, and he seemed to be making The Wave salute nonstop. If this kept up for much longer he was going to have one sore arm, he thought.

Further down the hall, Brad and Eric were standing at a table handing out **mimeographed pamphlets** and shouting, "Strength Through Discipline, Strength Through Community, Strength Through Action."

"Learn all about The Wave," Brad was telling passing students. "Here's a pamphlet."

"And don't forget the Wave rally this afternoon," Eric reminded them. "Work together and achieve your goals."

Ben smiled wearily. The **untethered energy** of these kids was tiring him out. There were Wave posters all over school now. Every single Wave member seemed to be involved in some activity—**recruiting new members**,

....

come into focus become more clear
mimeographed pamphlets copies of booklets
untethered energy constant activity
recruiting new members getting more people to join

disseminating information, preparing the gym for the rally that afternoon. Ben found it almost overwhelming.

A little further down the hall Ben had a funny sensation and stopped. He felt as if he was being followed. A few feet behind him stood Robert, smiling. Ben smiled back and kept going, but a few seconds later he stopped again. Robert was still behind him.

"Robert, what are you doing?" Mr. Ross asked.

"Mr. Ross, I'm **your bodyguard**," Robert announced.

"My what?"

Robert hesitated slightly. "I want to be your bodyguard," he said. "I mean, you're the leader, Mr. Ross; I can't let anything happen to you."

"What could happen to me?" Ben asked, startled by the notion.

But Robert seemed to ignore that question. "I know you need a bodyguard," he insisted. "I could do it, Mr. Ross. For the first time in my life I feel . . . well, nobody makes jokes about me anymore. I feel like I'm part of something special."

Ben nodded.

"So can't I do it?" Robert asked. "I know you need a bodyguard. I could do it, Mr. Ross."

....

disseminating giving out
your bodyguard the person who protects you

Ben looked into Robert's face. Where there had once been a **withdrawn and unconfident** boy, there now stood a serious Wave member, concerned for his leader. But a bodyguard? Ben hesitated a moment. Wasn't that going a little too far? More and more he'd begun to recognize the position of importance his students were unconsciously forcing upon him—the ultimate leader of The Wave. Several times over the last few days he had heard Wave members discussing "orders" he had given: orders to put posters up in the halls, orders to organize The Wave movement in the lower grades, even the order to change the pep rally into a Wave rally.

Except the crazy thing was, he'd never given those orders. Somehow they'd simply **evolved** in the students' imaginations, and once there, they automatically assumed he'd given them. It was as if The Wave had taken on a life of its own and now he and his students **were literally riding it**. Ben Ross looked at Robert Billings. Somewhere in his mind he knew that by agreeing to let Robert be his bodyguard, he was also agreeing to become a person who required a bodyguard. But wasn't that what the experiment required as well? "All right, Robert," he said. "You can be

....

withdrawn and unconfident shy, lonely, and insecure
evolved developed
were literally riding it could not stop The Wave from growing and becoming a powerful group

my bodyguard."

A wide smile appeared on Robert's face. Ben winked at him and continued down the hall. Perhaps having a bodyguard would be helpful. It was **essential** to the experiment that he **maintain the image of** leader of The Wave. Having a bodyguard could only **enhance** that image.

....

essential necessary

maintain the image of continue to act as the

enhance help, strengthen

BEFORE YOU MOVE ON...

1. **Inference** Why do you think the writer of Laurie's letter chooses to remain unknown?

2. **Comparisons** Reread page 118. How has Robert changed since The Wave began?

LOOK AHEAD Will Laurie's friends start to dislike her? Read pages 121–146 to find out.

CHAPTER 12

The Wave rally would be in the gym, but Laurie Saunders stood by her locker, uncertain that she wanted to go. She still **couldn't put into words exactly what bothered her about The Wave**, but she could feel it growing inside her. Something was wrong. The anonymous letter that morning was **a symptom**. It wasn't only that a senior had tried to bully a junior into joining The Wave. It was more—the fact that the junior hadn't put his name on the letter, the fact that he'd been afraid to. It was something Laurie herself had been trying to deny for days, but it just wouldn't go away. The Wave was scary. Oh, it was just great if you were an unquestioning member. But if you weren't . . .

....

couldn't put into words exactly what bothered her about The Wave could not really explain why The Wave scared her and made her feel uncomfortable

a symptom another reason that she was uncertain about joining The Wave

Laurie's thoughts were interrupted by a sudden flurry of shouts out in the quadrangle. She quickly went to a window and saw that two boys were fighting while a crowd of kids stood watching and yelling at them. Laurie gasped. One of the fighters was Brian Ammon! She watched as they threw punches at each other and then awkwardly wrestled to the ground. **What in the world?**

Now a teacher ran out and separated the two fighters. Grabbing each tightly by the arm, he started tugging them inside, no doubt to Principal Owens's office. As he went, Brian shouted, "Strength Through Discipline! Strength Through Community! Strength Through Action!"

The other boy shouted back, "Aw, **shove it**."

"You see that?"

The sudden sound of a voice so close to her startled Laurie, and she jumped around to find David beside her.

"I hope Principal Owens lets Brian attend The Wave rally after this," David said.

"Were they fighting about The Wave?" Laurie asked.

David shrugged. "It's more than that. That kid Brian was fighting, he's this junior named Deutsch who's been after Brian's position all year. **This thing's been brewing** for

....

What in the world? Why were they fighting?
shove it keep your ideas to yourself
This thing's been brewing They have been arguing

weeks. I just hope he got what he deserved."

"But Brian was shouting The Wave motto," Laurie said.

"Well, sure. He's really into it. We all are."

"Even the kid he was fighting?"

David shook his head. "Naw, Deutsch is a jerk, Laurie. If he was in The Wave he wouldn't be trying to steal Brian's position. That **guy's a real detriment to** the team. I wish Schiller would throw him off."

"Because he isn't in The Wave?" Laurie asked.

"Yeah," David replied. "If he really wanted **the best for the team** he'd join The Wave instead of giving Brian such a hard time. He's a one-man team, Laurie. **He's just on a big ego trip** and he's not helping anyone." David looked down the hall at a clock. "Come on, we've got to get to that rally. It's gonna start in a second."

Suddenly Laurie made a decision. "I'm not going," she said.

"What?" David looked shocked. "Why not?"

"Because I don't want to."

"Laurie, this is an incredibly important rally," David said. "All the new members of The Wave are going to be there."

"David, I think you and everyone else are taking this

....

guy's a real detriment to guy causes problems for
the best for the team the team to start winning
He's just on a big ego trip He thinks he is the best

whole Wave thing a little bit too seriously."

David shook his head. "No, I'm not. You're not taking this seriously enough. Look, Laurie, you've always been a leader. The other kids, they've always **looked up to you**. You've got to be at that rally."

"But that's exactly why I'm not going," Laurie tried to explain. "Let them make up their own minds about The Wave. They're individuals. They don't need me to help them."

"I don't understand you," David said.

"David, I can't believe how crazy everybody's gotten. The Wave is taking over everything."

"Sure," David said. "Because The Wave makes sense, Laurie. It works. Everybody's on the same team. Everybody's equal for once."

"Oh, that's terrific," Laurie said sarcastically. "Do we all **score a touchdown**?"

David stepped back and studied his girlfriend. He hadn't expected anything like this. Not from Laurie.

"Don't you see," Laurie said, mistaking his hesitation for **a glimmer of doubt**. "You're so idealistic, David. You're so intent on creating some kind of **utopian Wave society**

....

looked up to you wanted to be like you
score a touchdown become winners
a glimmer of doubt mistrust
utopian Wave society perfect world

full of equal people and great football teams that you don't see it at all. It can't happen, David. There will always be a few people who won't want to join. They have a right not to join."

David squinted at his girlfriend. "You know," he said, "you're just against this thing because you're not special anymore. Because you're not the best and most popular student in the class now."

"That's not true and you know it!" Laurie gasped.

"I think it is true!" David insisted. "Now you know how the rest of us felt listening to you always giving the right answers. Always being the best. How does it feel not to be the best anymore?"

"David, you're being stupid!" Laurie yelled at him.

David nodded. "All right, if I'm so stupid, why don't you go find yourself a smart boyfriend." He turned and walked away toward the gym.

Laurie stood behind and watched him. It's crazy, she thought. **Everything is going out of control.**

From what Laurie could hear, The Wave rally was a giant success. She was spending the period in the publications office down the hall. It was the only place she

....

Everything is going out of control. Everyone is changing so quickly, and I can not stop it or understand it.

could think of going where she would be safe from the questioning looks of kids wondering why she wasn't at the rally. Laurie did not want to admit that she was hiding, but it was true. That was how crazy this whole thing had become. You had to hide if you weren't part of it.

Laurie took out a pen and chewed on it nervously. She had to do something. *The Grapevine* had to do something.

A few minutes later the turning of the doorknob shook her from her thoughts. Laurie caught her breath. Had someone come to get her?

The door opened and Alex bopped in to the beat of the music coming through his earphones.

Laurie sank back in her chair and let out a big sigh.

When Alex saw Laurie he smiled and pulled the earphones off his head. "Hey, how come you're not **in with the troops**?"

Laurie shook her head. "Alex, it's not *that* bad."

But Alex just grinned. "Oh yeah? Pretty soon they're gonna have to change the name of this school to **Fort Gordon High**."

"**I'm not amused**, Alex," Laurie said.

Alex scrunched up his shoulders and made a face.

....

in with the troops at the rally with everyone else
Fort Gordon High the name of an army base
I'm not amused That is not funny

"Laurie, you must learn that nothing is above ridicule."

"Well, if you think they're troopers, aren't you frightened of being **drafted**, too?" Laurie asked.

Alex grinned. "Who, me?" Than he swiped through the air with several fierce-looking karate chops. "Anyone hassles me and I'll **Kung Foo them into chopped suey**."

The door of the publications office opened again and now Carl slipped in. Seeing Laurie and Alex there, he smiled. "Looks like I've **stumbled into Anne Frank's attic**," he said.

"The last of the rugged individuals," Alex said.

Carl nodded. "I believe it. I just came from the rally."

"They let you out?" Alex asked.

"I had to go to the bathroom," Carl answered.

"Hey, man," Alex said. "You got the wrong place."

Carl grinned. "This is where I went after the bathroom. Anyplace but that rally."

"Join the club," Laurie said.

"Maybe we should give ourselves a name," Alex said. "If they're The Wave, we could be The Ripple."

"What do you think?" Carl asked.

"About calling ourselves The Ripple?" Laurie said.

....

drafted forced to join

Kung Foo them into chopped suey fight them using martial arts so I will not have to join The Wave

stumbled into Anne Frank's attic found a safe place to hide from the members of The Wave

"No, about The Wave."

"I think it's time we put out that issue of *The Grapevine*," Laurie said.

"Excuse me for **injecting my own not always serious opinion**," Alex said, "but I think we ought to put it out fast before the rest of the staff **gets carried away by** The Mighty Wave."

"Pass the word around to the other staff members," Laurie said. "On Sunday at two o'clock we'll have an emergency meeting at my house. And try to make sure only non-Wave members are there."

That night Laurie stayed alone in her room. All afternoon she'd been too preoccupied with The Wave to allow herself to feel anything about David. Besides, they'd had fights before. But earlier in the week David had made a date to take her out that night, and here it was ten-thirty. It was obvious he wasn't coming, but Laurie couldn't quite believe it. They'd been going together since sophomore year and suddenly something as **trivial** as The Wave had broken them up—only The Wave wasn't trivial. Not anymore.

Several times during the evening Mrs. Saunders had

....

injecting my own not always serious opinion saying what I think

gets carried away by will only write about the ideas of

trivial unimportant, small

come up to her room to ask if she wanted to talk about it, but Laurie said she didn't. Her mother was such a worry-wart, and the problem was that this time there really was something worth worrying about. Laurie had been sitting at her desk trying to write something about The Wave for *The Grapevine*, but so far the page of paper before her was empty, except for a few water marks where a tear or two had fallen.

There were knocks on her door, and Laurie quickly wiped her eyes with the palm of her hands. It was no use; if her mother came in she'd see that she was crying. "I don't want to talk, Mom," she said.

But the door had started to open anyway. "It's not your mom, babe."

"Dad?" Laurie was surprised to see her father. It wasn't that she didn't feel close to him, but unlike her mother, he usually **didn't get involved in her problems**. Unless they somehow concerned golf.

"Can I come in?" her father asked.

"Well, Dad"—Laurie smiled slightly—"considering the fact that you're already in . . ."

Mr. Saunders nodded. "I'm sorry to **barge in**, babe, but your mother and I are both worried."

....

didn't get involved in her problems did not talk to her about problems at school or with boys

barge in come in suddenly

"She told you David broke up with me?" Laurie asked.

"Uh, yes, she did," Mr. Saunders said. "And I'm sorry about that, babe, I really am. I thought he was a nice boy."

"He was," Laurie said. Until The Wave, she thought.

"But, uh, I'm concerned about something else, Laurie. About something I heard on the golf course this evening." Mr. Saunders always left work early on Fridays to play nine holes of golf in a twilight league before the sun went down.

"What, Dad?"

"Today after school a boy was beaten up," her father said. "Now I got this story secondhand, so I don't know if it's all accurate. But apparently there was some kind of rally at school today, and he had resisted joining this Wave game or said something **critical** about it."

Laurie was speechless.

"The boy's parents are neighbors of one of the men I play golf with. They just moved in this year. So the boy must have been new at school."

"It sounds like he would have been **a perfect candidate for joining** The Wave," Laurie said.

"Maybe," said Mr. Saunders. "But Laurie, the boy is Jewish. Could that have **had anything to do with it**?"

....

critical negative

a perfect candidate for joining someone who would want to join

had anything to do with it been the reason he was beaten up

Laurie's jaw dropped. "You don't think . . . Dad, you can't believe **there's anything like that going on**. I mean, I don't like The Wave, but it's not like that, Dad, I swear it isn't."

"Are you sure?" Mr. Saunders asked.

"Well, I, uh, I know everyone who was originally in The Wave. I was there when it began. The whole idea was to show how something like Nazi Germany could have happened. It wasn't for us to become little Nazis. It's . . . it's—"

"It sounds like it's gotten out of hand, Laurie," her father said. "Has it?"

Laurie just nodded. She was too shocked to be able to say anything.

"Some of the men were talking about going to the school on Monday to talk to the principal," Mr. Saunders said. "Just, you know, to be on the safe side."

Laurie nodded. "We're going to put out a special issue of *The Grapevine*. We're going to **expose this whole thing**."

Her father was quiet for a few moments. "That sounds like a good idea, babe. But be careful, okay?"

"I will, Dad," Laurie said. "I promise."

....

Laurie's jaw dropped. Laurie was shocked.

there's anything like that going on members do not like people because of their religion or race

expose this whole thing tell people what The Wave is really like

CHAPTER 13

For the last three years during football season, sitting with Amy at Saturday afternoon games had become a habit for Laurie. David, of course, was on the team, and while Amy didn't have a steady boyfriend, the guys she dated were almost always football players. By Saturday afternoon, Laurie couldn't wait to see Amy; she had to tell her what she'd learned. It had surprised Laurie that Amy had gone along with The Wave so far, but now Laurie was certain that as soon as Amy learned about the boy who was beaten up, she would quickly **come to her senses**. Besides, Laurie sorely needed to talk to her about David. She still couldn't understand how something as dumb as The Wave could have made David **break up with her**. Maybe Amy knew

....

come to her senses realize The Wave was scary
break up with her not want to date her anymore

something she didn't know. Perhaps she could even talk to David for her.

Laurie got to the game just as it was starting. **It was by far the best turnout of the year**, and it took Laurie a moment to **spot Amy's head of curly blond hair** in the crowded bleachers. She was way up, almost at the top row. Laurie hurried to an aisle and was about to start up when someone yelled, "Stop!"

Laurie stopped and saw Brad coming toward her. "Oh, hi, Laurie, I didn't recognize you from behind," he said. Then he did The Wave salute.

Laurie just stood there without moving.

Brad frowned. "Come on, Laurie, just give me the salute and you can go up."

"What are you talking about, Brad?"

"You know, The Wave salute."

"You mean I can't go up into the stands unless I give The Wave salute?" Laurie asked.

Brad looked around sheepishly. "Well, that's what they decided, Laurie."

"Who are they?" Laurie asked.

"The Wave, Laurie, you know."

....

It was by far the best turnout of the year There were more people at the game than ever before

spot Amy's head of curly blond hair find Amy

"Brad, I thought *you* were The Wave. You're in Mr. Ross's class," Laurie said.

Brad shrugged. "I know. Look, **what's the big deal**? Just give me the salute and you can go up."

Laurie looked up at the crowded stands. "You mean everyone in the stands gave you the salute?"

"Well, yeah. In this part of the stands."

"Well, I want to go up and I don't want to give The Wave salute," Laurie said angrily.

"But you can't," Brad replied.

"Who says I can't?" Laurie asked loudly. Several students near them looked in their direction.

Brad blushed. "Look, Laurie," he said in a low voice. "Just do the stupid salute already."

But Laurie was adamant. "No, this is ridiculous. Even you know it's ridiculous."

Brad squirmed slightly. Then he looked around again and said, "Okay, don't salute, just go ahead. I don't think anyone's looking."

But all at once Laurie didn't want to join the people in the stands. **She had no intention of sneaking anywhere to join The Wave.** This whole thing had just gone insane.

....

what's the big deal what is wrong with giving the salute

She had no intention of sneaking anywhere to join The Wave. She did not want to pretend to be a part of The Wave.

Even some of The Wave members like Brad knew it was insane. "Brad," she said. "Why are you **doing this** if you know it's stupid? Why are you a part of it?"

"Look, Laurie, I can't talk about it now," Brad said. "The game's starting, I'm supposed to let people into the stands. I got too much to do."

"Are you afraid?" Laurie asked. "Are you afraid of what the other Wave members will do if you don't go along with them?"

Brad's mouth opened, but for a few seconds no sounds came out. "I'm not afraid of anyone, Laurie," he said finally. "And you better **shut your mouth**. You know, a lot of people noticed that you weren't at The Wave rally yesterday."

"So? So what?" Laurie demanded.

"I'm not saying anything, I'm just telling you," Brad said.

Laurie was **aghast**. She wanted to know what he was trying to say, but there was a big play on the field. Brad turned away, and her words were lost in the roar of the crowd.

Sunday afternoon Laurie and some of the staff of *The Grapevine* turned the Saunders' living room into a newsroom

....

doing this doing what The Wave tells you to do
shut your mouth stop saying bad things about The Wave
aghast shocked

as they put together a special edition of the paper devoted almost entirely to The Wave. Several members of the newspaper were not there, and when Laurie asked those present why, they seemed reluctant to answer at first. Then Carl said, "I have a feeling a few of our comrades would prefer not to **incur the wrath of The Wave**."

Laurie looked around the room at the other staffers, who were nodding in agreement with **Carl's assessment**.

"Sniveling, spineless amoebas," Alex shouted, jumping to his feet and raising his fist above his head. "I pledge to fight The Wave until the end. Give me liberty, or give me acne!"

He looked around at the puzzled faces. "Well," he explained, "I figured acne was worse than death."

"Sit down, Alex," someone said.

Alex sat and the group returned to the job of putting together the newspaper. But Laurie could sense that they were all acutely aware of the absent members.

The special edition on The Wave would include the story by the anonymous junior, and a report Carl had done on the sophomore who'd been beaten up.

It turned out that the boy had not been hurt badly, only **roughed up by a couple of hoods**. There was even some

....

incur the wrath of The Wave make members angry

Carl's assessment what Carl said

roughed up by a couple of hoods frightened by a couple of tough kids

uncertainty over whether it was over The Wave, or whether The Wave was just an excuse the hoods had used to start a fight. However, one of the hoods had **called the boy a dirty Jew**. The boy's parents told Carl they were keeping him out of school and planned to visit Principal Owens personally Monday morning.

There were other interviews with worried parents and concerned teachers. But the most critical article was an editorial Laurie had spent most of Saturday writing. It **condemned The Wave as a dangerous** and mindless movement that **suppressed** freedom of speech and thought and ran against everything the country was founded on. She pointed out that The Wave had already begun to do more harm than good (even with The Wave, the Gordon High Gladiators had lost to Clarkstown 42 to 6) and warned that unless it was stopped it would do much worse.

Carl and Alex said they'd take the paper to the printer first thing the next morning. The paper would be out by lunchtime.

....

called the boy a dirty Jew said terrible things to the boy about his race and religion

condemned The Wave as a dangerous said that The Wave was a wrong, dangerous,

suppressed did not allow

CHAPTER 14

There was one thing Laurie had to do before the paper came out. Monday morning she had to find Amy and explain to her about the story. She still hoped that as soon as Amy read it, she would **see The Wave for what it was** and change her mind about it. Laurie wanted to warn her in advance so she could get out of The Wave in case there was trouble.

She found Amy in the school library and gave her a copy of the editorial to read. As Amy read, **her mouth began to open wider and wider**. Finally she looked up at Laurie. "What are you going to do with it?"

"I'm publishing it in the paper," Laurie said.

"But you can't say these things about The Wave,"

....

see The Wave for what it was understand that The Wave was dangerous

her mouth began to open wider and wider she looked more and more shocked

Amy said.

"Why not?" Laurie asked. "They're true. Amy, The Wave **has become an obsession with everyone**. No one is thinking for themselves anymore."

"Oh, come on, Laurie," Amy said. "You're just upset. You're letting your fight with David get to you."

Laurie shook her head. "Amy, I'm serious. The Wave is hurting people. And everyone's going along with it **like a flock of sheep**. I can't believe that after reading this you'd still be part of it. Don't you see what The Wave is? It's everybody forgetting who they are. It's like *Night of the Living Dead* or something. Why do you want to be part of it?"

"Because it means that nobody is better than anyone else for once," Amy said. "Because ever since we became friends all I've ever done is try to compete with you and keep up with you. But now I don't feel like I have to have a boyfriend on the football team like you. And if I don't want to, I don't have to get the same grades you get, Laurie. For the first time in three years I feel like I don't have to keep up with Laurie Saunders and people will still like me."

Laurie felt chills run down her arms. "I, I, uh, always

....

has become an obsession with everyone is the only thing anyone is talking about

like a flock of sheep without thinking; blindly

Night of the Living Dead a horror movie

knew you felt that way," she stammered. "I always wanted to talk to you about it."

"Don't you know that half the parents in school say to their kids, 'Why can't you be like Laurie Saunders'?" Amy asked. "Come on, Laurie, the only reason you're against The Wave is because it means you're not **a princess** anymore."

Laurie was stunned. Even her best friend, someone as smart as Amy, was turning against her because of The Wave. It made her angry. "Well, I'm publishing this," she said.

Amy only looked up at her and said, "Don't, Laurie."

But Laurie shook her head. "I already have," she said. "And I know what I have to do."

Suddenly it was as if she was a stranger. Amy looked at her watch. "I gotta go," she said, and walked away, leaving Laurie standing alone in the library.

Copies of *The Grapevine* had never been **scooped** up faster than they were that day. The **school was abuzz with** the news. Very few kids had heard about the sophomore who was beaten up, and of course no one had heard the story by the anonymous junior before. But as soon as those stories appeared in the paper, other stories began to

....

a princess better than everyone
scooped picked
school was abuzz with students were talking about

circulate. Stories of threats and abuse directed at kids who, for one reason or another, had **resisted** The Wave.

There were other rumors going around, too, that teachers and parents had been to Principal Owens's office all morning complaining, and that the school counselors had begun interviewing students. There was **an air of unease** in the halls and classrooms.

In the faculty lounge, Ben Ross put down his copy of *The Grapevine* and rubbed his temples with his fingers. Suddenly he'd gotten a terrible headache. Something had gone wrong and somewhere in his mind Ross suspected that he was to blame for it. The roughing up of this boy was terrible, unbelievable. How could he justify an experiment that had such effects?

He was also surprised to find himself disturbed by the football team's embarrassing defeat by Clarkstown. It seemed odd to him that although he didn't care the least about high school athletics, this defeat would bother him so. Was it because of The Wave? During the last week he had begun to believe that if the football team **fared** well it would be a strong argument for the success of The Wave.

But since when did he want The Wave to succeed? The

....

circulate spread
resisted not joined
an air of unease a nervous feeling
fared played

success or failure of The Wave was not the point of the experiment. He was supposed to be interested in what his students learned from The Wave, not in The Wave itself.

There was a medicine chest in the faculty lounge, stocked with just about every brand of aspirin and nonaspirin headache **remedy** that had ever been invented. A friend of his had once remarked that while doctors as a group suffered from the highest incidence of suicide, teachers had to have the highest incidence of headaches. Ben shook three tablets from a bottle and headed for the door to get some water.

But just as he reached the faculty room door, Ben stopped. Outside in the hall he could hear voices—Norm Schiller's and another male voice he didn't recognize. Someone must have stopped Norm just as he was going into the faculty lounge and now he stood outside the door talking. Ben listened from inside.

"No, it wasn't worth a damn," Schiller was saying. "Sure it got them **psyched up**, made 'em think they could win. But out on the field they couldn't **execute**. All the waves in the world don't mean a thing next to a well-executed quarterback option. There's no substitute for learning the damn game."

....

remedy medicine
psyched up excited
execute perform the plays

"Ross really has these kids brainwashed if you ask me," the unidentified man said. "I don't know what the hell he thinks he's up to, but I don't like it. And none of the other teachers I've talked to do either. **Where does he get the right?**"

"Don't ask me," Schiller said.

The faculty room door began to open and Ben quickly backed away, pushing through a door into the small faculty bathroom that **adjoined** the lounge. His heart was pounding rapidly and his head hurt even more. He swallowed the three aspirins and avoided looking at himself in the mirror. Was he afraid of who he might see? A high school history teacher who had accidentally slipped into the role of a dictator?

David Collins still couldn't understand it. It didn't make sense to him why everyone hadn't joined The Wave in the first place. Then there never would have been these hassles. They all could have functioned as equals, as teammates. People were laughing and saying that The Wave didn't help the football team at all on Saturday, but what did they expect? The Wave **wasn't a miracle drug**. The team had

....

Where does he get the right? Why did he think he could start something like The Wave?

adjoined was next to

wasn't a miracle drug could not produce a miracle

known about The Wave for exactly five days before the game. What had changed was the team spirit and the team attitude.

David stood outside on the school lawn with Robert Billings and a bunch of other kids from Mr. Ross's class looking at *The Grapevine*. Laurie's story made him feel a little sick. He hadn't heard anything about anyone threatening or hurting anyone and for all he knew, she and her staff had made it all up. An unsigned letter and a story about a sophomore he'd never heard of. Okay, he was unhappy that Laurie refused to be part of The Wave. But why couldn't she and the people like her just leave The Wave alone? Why did they have to attack it?

Robert, beside him, was getting really upset over Laurie's story. "These are all lies," he said angrily. "She can't be allowed to say these things."

"It's not that important," David told him. "Nobody cares what Laurie's writing or what she has to say."

"Are you kidding?" Robert said. "Anyone who reads this **is going to get the completely wrong idea about The Wave**."

"I told her not to publish it," Amy said.

....

is going to get the completely wrong idea about The Wave will not understand The Wave and will think it is dangerous

"Hey, relax," David said. "There's no law that says people have to believe in what we're trying to do. But if we can keep making The Wave work, they'll see. They'll see all the good things it can do."

"Yeah, but if we don't watch out," Eric said, "these people are going to ruin it for the rest of us. Have you heard the rumors going around today? I heard there are parents and teachers and all kinds of people in Principal Owens's office complaining. Can you believe that? **At this rate** no one will get a chance to see what The Wave can do."

"Laurie Saunders is **a threat**," Robert stated bluntly. "She must be stopped."

David didn't like the **sinister** tone in Robert's voice. "Hey, wait—" he began to protest.

But Brian cut him off. "Don't worry, Robert, David and I can take care of Laurie, right, Dave?"

"Uh . . ." David suddenly felt Brian's hand on his shoulder slowly guiding him away from the rest of the group. Robert was nodding in approval.

"Look, man," Brian whispered. "If anyone can get Laurie to stop, you can."

"Yeah, but I don't like Robert's attitude," David hissed

....

At this rate If people keep complaining
a threat going to harm The Wave
sinister evil, scary

back. "It's like we must **wipe out** anyone who resists us. That's the exact opposite of how we should approach this."

"Dave, listen. Robert is just a little overenthusiastic sometimes. But you have to **admit he has a point**. If Laurie keeps writing stuff like this, The Wave won't have a chance. Just tell her to **cool it**, Dave. She'll listen to you."

"I don't know, Brian."

"Look, we'll wait for her after school tonight. Then you can go talk to her, okay?"

David nodded reluctantly. "I guess."

....

wipe out destroy
admit he has a point agree that he might be right
cool it stop writing

BEFORE YOU MOVE ON...

1. **Plot** On pages 123–125, Laurie and David get into a fight about The Wave. Why?

2. **Cause and Effect** What happens after Laurie prints her critical editorial about The Wave in the school newspaper?

   LOOK AHEAD Read pages 147–166 to see how Laurie handles the attacks against her.

CHAPTER 15

Christy Ross was in a hurry to get home after choir that afternoon. Ben had disappeared from school halfway through the day, and she had a feeling she knew why. When she got home she found her husband hunched over a book on Nazi youth. "What happened to you today?" she asked.

Without looking up from his book, Ben answered irritably, "I left early. I, uh, wasn't feeling well. But I need to be alone now, Chris. I have to be prepared for tomorrow."

"But honey, I need to talk to you," Christy **implored**.

"Can't it wait?" Ben snapped. "I've got to finish this before class tomorrow."

"No," Christy insisted. "That's what I have to talk to you about. This Wave thing. Have you any idea what's going

----

implored pleaded, urged

on at school, Ben? I mean, let's not even **dwell on** the fact that half my class has been skipping just to go to yours. Do you realize that this Wave of yours is **disrupting the entire school**? At least three teachers stopped me in the hall today to ask what the hell you're up to. And they're complaining to the principal too."

"I know, I know. And that's because they just don't understand what I'm trying to do," Ben answered.

"Are you serious, Ben?" his wife asked. "Did you know that the school counselors have begun questioning students in your class?" his wife asked. "Are you sure *you* know what you're doing? Because frankly, no one else in school thinks you do."

"Don't you think I know that?" Ben replied. "I know what they're saying about me. **That I'm crazy with power** . . . that I'm on an ego trip."

"Have you thought that they may be right?" Christy asked. "I mean, think of your original goals. Are they still the same ones you have now?"

Ben ran his hands through his hair. He already had enough problems with The Wave. "Christy, I thought you were on my side." But inside, he knew that she was right.

....

dwell on think about

disrupting the entire school distracting everyone; changing everything

That I'm crazy with power That I think I am powerful

"I am on your side, Ben," his wife answered. "But I've seen you these last few days and it's like I don't even know you. You've become so involved in **playing this role** at school that you're starting to **slip into it** at home. I've seen you **go overboard** like this before, Ben. Now you've got to turn it off, honey."

"I know. It must look to you like I've gone too far. But I can't stop now." He shook his head wearily. "Not yet."

"Then when?" Christy asked angrily. "After you or some of these kids do something you'll all regret?"

"Do you think I'm not aware of that?" Ben asked. "Do you think it doesn't worry me? But I created this experiment, and they went along. If I stop now they'll all be left **hanging**. They'd be confused, and they wouldn't have learned anything."

"Well, let them be confused," Christy said.

Ben suddenly jumped to his feet in frustrated anger. "No, I won't do that. I can't do that!" he shouted at his wife. "I'm their teacher. I was responsible for getting them into this. I admit that maybe I did let this go too long. But they've come too far to just drop it now. I have to push them until they get the point. I might be teaching these kids the

---

playing this role acting like a powerful leader
slip into it act like that
go overboard get too involved in something
hanging without a leader and without a movement

most important lesson of their lives!"

Christy was not impressed. "Well, I just hope Principal Owens agrees with you, Ben," she told him. "Because he caught me as I was leaving today and said he'd been looking for you all day. He wants to see you first thing tomorrow morning."

The Grapevine staff stayed late after school that day to celebrate their victory. The issue on The Wave had been so successful that it was almost impossible to find an extra copy anywhere. Not only that, but teachers and administrators and even some students had been stopping them all day and thanking them for revealing "the other side" of The Wave. Already they had heard stories that some students were **resigning from** The Wave.

The staff had realized that a single issue of the paper was not enough to stop a movement that had gained as much momentum as The Wave had that past week. But at least they had **struck it a serious blow**. Carl said he doubted there would be any more incidents of threats against non-Wave members—or any more beatings.

As usual, Laurie was the last one to leave the publications

----

resigning from leaving
struck it a serious blow seriously hurt the movement

office. One thing about *The Grapevine* staff—they were great party-ers, but when it came time to clean up somehow they all disappeared. It had come as a shock to Laurie earlier that year when she realized what having the top position on the paper, editor-in-chief, really meant: having to do every little stupid job no one else wanted to do. And tonight that meant cleaning up after the rest of the staff went home.

By the time she finished, Laurie realized that it had already grown dark out, and she was practically alone in the school building. As she closed the door of *The Grapevine* office and turned off the light, that nervousness she'd felt all week began to return again. The Wave **was undoubtedly smarting from the wounds** *The Grapevine* **had inflicted**, but it was still strong in Gordon High, and Laurie was aware that as the head of the paper, she . . . no, she told herself, you're just being silly and paranoid. The Wave was nothing serious, just a classroom experiment that had gotten slightly out of hand. There was nothing to be afraid of.

The corridors were darkened now as Laurie headed to her locker to drop off a book she would not need that evening. The silence of the empty school was **eerie**. For the first time she heard sounds she'd never heard before:

....

was undoubtedly smarting from the wounds *The Grapevine* **had inflicted** had definitely been hurt by the articles and criticism of it in the newspaper

eerie creepy, scary

the hums and buzzes of electrical current running to and from alarms and smoke detectors. A bubbling, splashing sound coming from the science room where some overnight experiment must **have been left brewing**. Even the unusually loud, hollow echo of her own shoes as they rapped the hard corridor floors.

A few feet from her locker, Laurie **froze**. There on her locker door, the word "enemy" was painted in red letters. Suddenly the loudest noise in the corridor was the quick, insistent beating of her own heart. Calm down, she told herself. Someone is just trying to scare you. She tried to get control of herself and started to do the combination of her lock. But she stopped in midturn. Had she heard something? Footsteps?

Laurie backed slowly away from her locker, **gradually losing her battle to suppress her own growing fright**. She turned and started walking down the hallway toward the exit. The sound of footsteps seemed to be growing louder, and Laurie quickened her pace. The footsteps grew even louder, and all at once the lights at the far end of the hall went out. Terrified, Laurie turned and peered back down into the dark hallway. Was that someone? Was there

....

have been left brewing be still going

froze stopped

gradually losing her battle to suppress her own growing fright becoming more terrified

someone down there?

The next thing Laurie knew she was running down the hallway toward the exit doors at the end. It seemed to take forever to get there, and when she finally reached the double metal doors and **banged her hip against the opening bar**, they were locked!

In a panic, Laurie threw herself against the next set of doors. Miraculously they opened, and she flew out into the cool evening air, running and running.

It seemed as if she ran for a long time, and finally she lost her breath and had to slow down, clutching her books to her breast and breathing hard. She felt safer now.

David sat waiting in the passenger seat of Brian's van. They were parked near the all-night tennis courts because David knew that when Laurie came home from school after dark she always **took this route**, where the bright lights from the courts made her feel safe. For almost an hour now they had been sitting in the van. Brian was in the driver's seat, keeping his eye on the sideview mirror watching for Laurie, and whistling some song so out of tune that David had no idea what it was. David watched the tennis players

....

banged her hip against the opening bar tried to open the doors

took this route walked this way

and listened to the monotonous **plunk-ka-plunk** of tennis balls being hit back and forth.

"Brian, can I ask you a question?" David said after a long while.

"What?"

"What are you whistling?"

Brian seemed surprised. "'Take Me Out to the Ball Game,'" he said. Then he whistled a few more bars. Coming from his lips, the song seemed completely unrecognizable. "There, now can you tell?"

David nodded. "Sure, Brian, sure." He went back to watching the tennis players.

A moment later, Brian sat up in his seat. "Hey, here she comes."

David turned and looked down the block. Laurie was coming down the sidewalk, walking quickly. He reached for the door handle. "Okay, now just let me take care of this alone," he said, pulling the handle.

"Just as long as she understands," Brian said. **"We're not playing around anymore."**

"Sure, Brian," David said and got out of the van. Now Brian was starting to sound like Robert, too.

....

plunk-ka-plunk sound

"We're not playing around anymore." "We're serious about The Wave, and she needs to stop criticizing it."

He had to jog to catch up with her, all the while uncertain of **how he should handle this**. All he knew was that it was better that he do it than Brian. He reached her, but Laurie did not stop, and he had to walk quickly to keep up with her.

"Hey, Laurie, can't you wait up?" he asked. "I've got to talk to you. It's real important."

Laurie slowed down and glanced behind him.

"It's okay, nobody else is coming," David said.

Laurie stopped. David noticed she was breathing hard and clutching her books tightly.

"Well, David," she said. "I'm not used to seeing you alone. Where are your troops?"

David knew he had to ignore her **antagonistic** remarks and try to **reason with her**. "Look, Laurie, will you just listen to me for a minute, please?"

But Laurie didn't seem interested. "David, we said everything we had to say to each other the other day. I don't want to **rehash** it now, so just leave me alone."

Against his will, David felt himself getting mad. She wouldn't even listen. "Laurie, you've got to stop writing stuff against The Wave. You're causing all kinds of problems."

....

how he should handle this what he should say
antagonistic angry
reason with her make her understand him
rehash say it again

"The Wave is causing the problems, David."

"It is not," David insisted. "Look Laurie, we want you with us, not against us."

Laurie shook her head. "Well, **count me out**. I told you, I quit. This is not a game anymore. People have been hurt."

She started to walk away, but David followed her. "That was an accident," he insisted. "Some guys just used The Wave as an excuse for beating that kid up. Don't you see? The Wave is still **for the good of the whole**. Why can't you see that, Laurie? It could be a whole new system. We could make it work."

"Not with me, you can't."

David knew if he didn't stop her she'd get away. It just wasn't fair that one person could **ruin it for everyone else**. He had to convince her. He had to! The next thing he knew, he had grabbed her arm.

"Let go of me!" Laurie struggled to get free, but David held her arm tightly.

"Laurie, you've got to stop," he said. It just wasn't fair.

"David, let go of my arm!"

"Laurie, stop writing those articles! Keep your mouth shut about The Wave! You're ruining it for everyone else!"

....

count me out I am not going to join The Wave

for the good of the whole good for everyone

ruin it for everyone else stop The Wave

But Laurie kept resisting. "I will write and I will say anything that I want to, and you can't stop me!" she yelled at him.

Overcome with anger, David grabbed her other arm. Why **did she have to be so stubborn**? Why couldn't she see how good The Wave could be? "We can stop you, and we will!" he shouted at her.

But Laurie only struggled harder to get out of his grasp. "I hate you!" she cried. "I hate The Wave! I hate all of you!"

The words struck David like a hard slap in the face. Almost out of control, he screamed "Shut up!" and threw her down on the grass. Her books went flying as she fell roughly to the ground.

David instantly **recoiled** in shock at what he had done. Laurie lay still on the ground and he was filled with fear as he dropped to his knees and put his arms around her. "Jeez, Laurie, are you all right?"

Laurie nodded, but seemed unable to talk **as sobs filled her throat**.

David held her tightly. "God, I'm sorry," he whispered. He could feel her tremble and he wondered how on earth

....

did she have to be so stubborn wouldn't she listen to him
recoiled stopped
as sobs filled her throat because she was crying so hard

he could have done something so stupid. What could have made him want to hurt the girl, the one he really still loved. Laurie pushed herself up slightly and sat sobbing and gasping for breath. David could not believe it. He felt almost as if he were **coming out of a trance**. What had **possessed** him these last days that could cause him to do something so stupid? There he'd been, denying that The Wave could hurt anyone, and at the same time he'd hurt Laurie, his own girlfriend, in the name of The Wave!

It was crazy—but David knew that he'd been wrong. Anything that could make him do what he'd just done was wrong. It had to be.

Meanwhile, moving slowly down the street, Brian's van passed them and disappeared into the darkness.

Later that night, Christy Ross went into the study where her husband was working. "Ben," she said firmly, "I'm sorry to interrupt you, but I've been thinking, and I have something important to say."

Ben leaned back in his chair and looked at his wife uneasily.

"Ben, you've got to end The Wave tomorrow," Christy

....

coming out of a trance waking up from a magic spell
possessed taken control of

told him. "I know how much this means to you and how important you think it is for your students. But I'm telling you it must end."

"How can you say that?" Ben asked.

"Because, Ben, if you don't end it I am convinced Principal Owens will," she told him. "And if he has to end it, I promise you your experiment will be a failure. I've been thinking all evening about what you've been trying to accomplish, Ben, and I think I'm beginning to understand. But did you ever consider, back when you began this experiment, what might happen if it didn't work? Did it ever occur to you that you're risking **your reputation** as a teacher? If this goes wrong, do you think parents are going to let their kids into your classroom again?"

"Don't you think you're exaggerating?" Ben asked.

"No," Christy replied. "Did it ever occur to you that you've not only put yourself **into jeopardy** but me as well? Some people think that just because I'm your wife that somehow I'm involved in this **Wave idiocy**, too. Does that seem fair, Ben? It breaks my heart that after two years at Gordon High you're in danger of ruining your job. You're going to end it tomorrow, Ben. You're going to go into

....

your reputation your job and what people think of you
into jeopardy at risk
Wave idiocy foolish movement

Principal Owens and tell him that it's over."

"Christy, how can you tell me what to do?" Ben asked. "How can I possibly end it in one day and still **do the students justice**?"

"You have to think of something, Ben," Christy insisted. "You just have to."

Ben rubbed his forehead and thought about the next morning's meeting with Principal Owens. Owens was a good man, and open to new ideas and experiments, but now he had immense pressures on him. On one side parents and teachers were **in arms** over The Wave, and pressure was growing on the principal to step in and **put a halt to** it. On the other side there was only Ben Ross, pleading with him not to interfere, trying to explain that to stop The Wave abruptly could be a disaster for the students. So much effort had gone into it. To end The Wave without explanation would be like reading the first half of a novel and not finishing it. But Christy was right. Ben knew The Wave had to end. The important thing wasn't when it ended, but how. The students had to end it themselves, and they had to understand why. Otherwise the lesson, the pain, all that had gone into it, was for nothing.

....

do the students justice make the students understand the experiment

in arms upset

put a halt to stop

"Christy," Ben said, "I know it should end, but I just don't **see how**."

His wife sighed wearily. "Are you saying that you're going to go into Principal Owens's office tomorrow morning and tell *him* that? That you know it should end but you don't know how? Ben, you're supposed to be The Wave's leader. You're the one they're supposed to follow **blindly**."

Ben did not appreciate the sarcasm in his wife's voice, but again he knew she was right. The students in The Wave had made him more of a leader than he had ever wished to be. But it was also true that he had not resisted. In fact, he had to admit that before the experiment had gone bad, he had enjoyed those **fleeting** moments of power. A crowded room full of students obeying his commands, the Wave symbol he'd created posted all over the school, even a bodyguard. He had read that power could **be seductive**, and now he had experienced it. Ben ran his hand through his hair. The members of The Wave were not the only ones who had to learn the lesson power taught. Their teacher did, as well.

"Ben?" Christy said.

"Yes, I know, I'm thinking," he replied. Wondering was more like it. Suppose there was something he could do

....

see how know how to end it
blindly without questioning you or your orders
fleeting short
be seductive make you do crazy things

tomorrow. Suppose he did something **abrupt and final**. Would they follow him? At once, Ben understood what he had to do. "Okay, Christy, I've got an idea."

His wife looked at him uncertainly. "Something you're sure will work?"

Ben shook his head. "No, but I hope it will," he said.

Christy nodded and looked at her watch. It was late and she was tired. She leaned over her husband and kissed him on the forehead. The skin was **damp with perspiration**. "You coming to bed?"

"Soon," he said.

After Christy went into the bedroom, Ben went over his plan again in his mind. It seemed **sound** and he stood up, determined to get some sleep. He was just shutting off the lights when the doorbell rang. Rubbing his eyes with weariness, Ross trudged to the front door.

"Who is it?"

"It's David Collins and Laurie Saunders, Mr. Ross."

Surprised, Ben pulled the door open. "What are you doing here?" he asked. "It's late."

"Mr. Ross, we've got to talk to you," David said. "It's real important."

....

abrupt and final shocking that would end it
damp with perspiration wet with sweat
sound good, right

"Well, come in and sit down," Ben said.

As David and Laurie entered the living room, Ben could see that both of them were **shaken up**. Had something even worse happened because of The Wave? **God forbid.** The two students sat down on the couch. David leaned forward.

"Mr. Ross, you've got to help us," he said, his voice filled with **agitation**.

"What is it?" Ben asked. "What's wrong?"

"It's The Wave," David said.

"Mr. Ross," said Laurie, "we know how important this is to you—but it's just gone too far."

Before Ross could even respond, David added, "It's taken over, Mr. Ross. You can't say anything **against it**. People are afraid to."

"The kids at school are scared," Laurie told him. "They're really scared. Not only to say anything against The Wave, but of what might happen to them if they don't go along with it."

Ben nodded. In a way, what these students were telling him relieved him of part of his concern about The Wave. If he did as Christy told him and thought back to the original goals of the experiment, then the fears Laurie and David spoke of confirmed that The Wave was a success. After all,

....

shaken up frightened, upset
God forbid. He hoped not.
agitation stress, worry
against it bad about it

The Wave had originally been **conceived** as a way to show these kids what life in Nazi Germany might have been like. Apparently, in terms of fear and **forced compliance**, it had been an overwhelming success—too much of a success.

"You can't even have a conversation without wondering who's listening," Laurie told him.

Ben could only nod again. He recalled those students in his own history classes who had condemned the Jews for not taking the Nazi threat seriously, for not fleeing their homes and ghettos when rumors of the concentration camps and gas chambers first **filtered back to** them. Of course, Ross thought, how could any rational person believe such a thing? And who could have believed that a nice bunch of high school students like those at Gordon High could have become a fascist group called The Wave? Was it a weakness of man that made him want to ignore the darker side of his fellow human beings?

David yanked him from his thoughts. "Tonight I almost hurt Laurie because of The Wave," he said. "I don't know what **came over me**. But I do know that it's the same thing that's come over almost everyone who's in The Wave."

"You've got to stop it," Laurie urged him.

....

conceived created
forced compliance being forced to obey
filtered back to reached
came over me made me want to act like that

"I know," Ben said. "I will."

"What are you going to do, Mr. Ross?" David asked.

Ben knew he could not reveal his plan to Laurie and David. It was essential that the members of The Wave decide the matter for themselves, and for the experiment to be a true success, Ben could only present them with the evidence. If David or Laurie went to school the next day and told the students that Mr. Ross planned to end The Wave, the students would **be biased**. They might end it without really understanding why it had to end. Or worse, they might try and fight him, keeping The Wave alive despite **its obvious destiny**.

"David, Laurie," he said, "you have discovered for yourselves what the other members of The Wave have not yet learned. I promise you that tomorrow I will try to help them toward that discovery. But I have to do it my way, and I can only ask that you trust me. Can you do that?"

David and Laurie nodded uncertainly as Ben rose and showed them to the door. "Come on, it's too late for you kids to be out," he told them. As they went through the door, however, Ben had another thought. "Listen, do either of you know two students who have never been involved in

....

be biased not listen to him as their leader
its obvious destiny knowing the dangerous outcome

The Wave? Two students who Wave members don't know and wouldn't miss?"

David considered for a moment. Amazing as it might be, almost everyone he knew in school had become a member of The Wave. But Laurie thought of two people. "Alex Cooper and Carl Block," she said. "They're on *The Grapevine* staff."

"Okay," Ben told them. "Now, I want both of you to go back to class tomorrow and act as if everything is fine. Pretend we haven't talked, and don't tell anyone that you were here tonight or that you spoke to me. Can you do that?"

David nodded, but Laurie looked concerned. "I don't know, Mr. Ross."

But Ben **cut her short**. "Laurie, it is extremely important that we do it this way. You must trust me. Okay?"

Reluctantly Laurie agreed. Ben **bade them** good-bye, and she and David stepped into the dark.

....

cut her short interrupted her
bade them said

BEFORE YOU MOVE ON...

1. **Cause and Effect** On page 157, what happens after David pushes Laurie to the ground?

2. **Argument** Reread pages 159–161. What reasons does Christy give to Ben that he should end the experiment?

LOOK AHEAD How will Mr. Ross stop The Wave? Read pages 167–189 to find out.

CHAPTER 16

The next morning in Principal Owens's office, Ben had to pull his handkerchief out of his pocket and pat the perspiration off his forehead. Across the desk, Principal Owens had just slammed his fist down. "Damn it, Ben! I don't care about your experiment. I've got teachers complaining, I've got parents calling me every five minutes wanting to know **what the hell's going on** here, what the hell are we doing with their kids. You think I can tell *them* it's an experiment? My God, man, you know that boy who was roughed up last week? **His rabbi** was here yesterday. The man spent two years in **Auschwitz**. Do you think he gives a damn about your experiment?"

Ben sat up in his chair. "Principal Owens, I understand

....

what the hell's going on what is happening
His rabbi The leader of his synagogue
Auschwitz a Nazi concentration camp

the pressure you're under. I know that The Wave went too far. I . . ." Ben took a deep breath. "I realize now that I made a mistake. A history class is not a science lab. You can't experiment with human beings. Especially high school students who aren't aware that they're part of an experiment. But for a moment let's forget that it was a mistake, that it went too far. Let's look at it right now. Right now there are two hundred students here who think The Wave is great. I can still teach them a lesson. All I need is the rest of the day, and I can teach them a lesson they will never forget."

Principal Owens looked at him **skeptically**. "And what do you expect me to tell their parents and the other teachers in the meantime?"

Ben patted his forehead with his handkerchief again. He knew he was taking a **gamble**, but what choice did he have? He had gotten them into this and he had to **get them out**. "Tell them that I promise it will all be over by tonight."

Principal Owens arched an eyebrow. "And exactly how do you intend to do that?"

It didn't take Ben long to outline his plan. Across the desk, Principal Owens tapped out his pipe and considered it. A long and uncomfortable silence followed. Finally he said,

....

skeptically uncertainly; not sure if he could believe him
gamble chance, risk
get them out stop it

"Ben, I'm going to be absolutely **straight** with you. This Wave thing has made Gordon High look very bad, and I'm very unhappy about it. I'll let you have today. But I have to warn you: If it doesn't work, I'm going to have to ask you **for your resignation**."

Ben nodded. "I understand," he said.

Principal Owens stood and offered his hand. "I hope you can make this work, Ben," he said solemnly. "You're a fine teacher and we'd hate to lose you."

Outside in the hall Ben had no time to dwell on Principal Owens's words. He had to find Alex Cooper and Carl Block, and he had to work fast.

In history class that day Ben waited until the students had come to attention. Then he said, "I have a special announcement about The Wave. At five o'clock today there will be a rally in the auditorium—for Wave members only."

David smiled to himself and winked at Laurie.

"The reason for the rally is the following," Mr. Ross continued. "The Wave is not just a classroom experiment. It's much, much more than that. **Unbeknownst to you**, starting last week, all across the country teachers like myself have been recruiting and training a **youth brigade** to show

....

straight direct, honest
for your resignation to quit your job
Unbeknownst to you Although you do not know
youth brigade a group of young people

the rest of the nation how to **achieve a better society**.

"As you know, this country has just gone through a decade in which steady **double-digit inflation** has severely weakened the economy," Mr. Ross continued. "**Unemployment has run chronically high**, and the crime rate has been worse than any time in memory. Never before has the morale of the United States been so low. Unless this trend is stopped, a growing number of people, including the founders of The Wave, believe that our country is doomed."

David was no longer smiling. This was not what he had expected to hear. Mr. Ross didn't seem to be ending The Wave at all. If anything, he seemed to be going more deeply into it than ever!

"We must prove that through discipline, community, and action we can turn this country around," Ross told the class. "Look what we have accomplished in this school alone in just a few days. If we can change things here, we can change things everywhere."

Laurie gave David a frightened look. Mr. Ross went on: "In factories, hospitals, universities—in all institutions—"

David jumped out of his chair in protest. "Mr. Ross,

....

achieve a better society improve the country

double-digit inflation increases in prices and a decline of what our money is worth

Unemployment has run chronically high The number of people who cannot find jobs is too high

Mr. Ross!"

"Sit down, David!" Mr. Ross ordered.

"But, Mr. Ross, you said—"

Ben cut him off urgently. "I said, sit down, David. Don't interrupt me."

David returned to his seat, unable to believe his ears as Mr. Ross continued, "Now listen carefully. During the rally the founder and national leader of The Wave will appear on cable television to announce the formation of a National Wave Youth Movement!"

All around them students started cheering. **It was too much for Laurie and David.** Both rose to their feet, this time to face the class.

"Wait, wait," David pleaded with them. "Don't listen to him. Don't listen. He's lying."

"Can't you see what he's doing?" Laurie said emotionally. "Can't any of you think for yourselves anymore?"

But the room only grew quiet as the class glared at them.

Ross knew he had to act quickly, before Laurie and David **revealed** too much. He realized he had made an error. He had asked Laurie and David to trust him, and he had not expected them to disobey. But instantly it made

....

It was too much for Laurie and David. Laurie and David knew they had to do something to stop Mr. Ross and The Wave.

revealed said

sense to him that they would. He snapped his fingers. "Robert, I want you to take over the class until I return from escorting David and Laurie to the principal's office."

"Mr. Ross, yes!"

Mr. Ross quickly walked to the classroom door and held it open for Laurie and David.

Outside in the hall, David and Laurie walked slowly toward the principal's office, followed by Mr. Ross. In the background they could hear steady, loud chants **emanating** from Mr. Ross's room: "Strength Through Discipline! Strength Through Community! Strength Through Action!"

"Mr. Ross, you lied to us last night," David said bitterly.

"No, I didn't, David. But I told you, you would have to trust me," Mr. Ross replied.

"Why should we?" Laurie asked. "You were the one who started The Wave in the first place."

The point was a good one. Ben could think of no reason why they should trust him. He only knew that they should. He hoped that by evening they would understand.

David and Laurie spent most of the afternoon waiting outside Principal Owens's office to see him. They were

....

emanating coming

The point was a good one. He realized they were right.

miserable and depressed, certain that Mr. Ross had tricked them into cooperating with him so that they could not prevent what now appeared to be the final hours before The Wave movement at Gordon High joined the national Wave movement, which had been growing **simultaneously** at high schools all over the country.

Even Principal Owens seemed unsympathetic when he finally got around to seeing them. On his desk was a brief report from Mr. Ross, and although neither of them could see what it said, it was obvious that it must have stated that Laurie and David had disrupted the class. Both of them pleaded with the principal to stop The Wave and the five o'clock rally, but Principal Owens only insisted that everything would be all right.

Finally he told them to go back to their classes. David and Laurie **were incredulous**. Here they were trying to prevent the worst thing they'd ever seen happen in school and Principal Owens seemed **to be oblivious**.

Out in the hall, David threw his books into his locker and slammed the door shut. "Forget it," he told Laurie angrily. "I'm not hanging around here anymore today. I'm **splitting**."

....

simultaneously at the same time
were incredulous could not believe what was happening
to be oblivious to not realize that The Wave was dangerous
splitting leaving

"Just wait for me to put my books away," Laurie told him. "I'll join you."

A few minutes later, as they walked down the sidewalk away from school, Laurie sensed that David was getting depressed. "I can't believe how dumb I was, Laurie," he kept saying. "I can't believe I really **fell for it**."

Laurie squeezed his hand. "You weren't dumb, David. You were idealistic. I mean, there were good things about The Wave. It couldn't be all bad, or no one would have joined in the first place. It's just that they don't see what's bad about it. They think it makes everyone equal, but they don't understand that it **robs you of your right to be independent**."

"Laurie, is it possible that we're wrong about The Wave?" David asked.

"No, David, we're right," Laurie answered.

"Then why doesn't anybody else see it?" he asked.

"I don't know. It's like they're all in a trance. They just won't listen anymore."

David nodded hopelessly.

It was still early and they decided to walk to a park nearby. Neither wanted to go home yet. David wasn't sure

....

fell for it believed in The Wave and joined it

robs you of your right to be independent takes away your freedom and ability to think for yourself

what to think of The Wave or Mr. Ross. Laurie still believed it was a fad that the kids would ultimately get bored with, no matter who organized it or where. What frightened her was what the kids in The Wave might do before they grew tired of it.

"I feel alone all of a sudden," David said as they walked through the trees in the park. "It's like all my friends are part of a crazy movement and I'm an outcast just because I refuse to be exactly like them."

Laurie knew exactly how he felt, because she felt it, too. She moved close to him and he put his arm around her. Laurie felt closer to David than ever. Wasn't it **odd** how going through something bad like this could bring them closer? She thought back to the night before, how David had forgotten entirely about The Wave the second he'd realized he'd hurt her. Suddenly she hugged him hard.

"What?" David was surprised.

"Oh, uh, nothing," she said.

"Hmmm." David looked away.

Laurie **felt her mind drifting back to** The Wave. She tried to imagine the school auditorium that afternoon,

....

odd strange
felt her mind drifting back to started thinking again about

filled with Wave members. And some leader somewhere speaking to them over the television. What would he tell them? To burn books? To force all non-Wave members to wear armbands? It seemed so **utterly** crazy that anything like this could happen. So . . . suddenly Laurie remembered something. "David," she said, "do you remember the day this all started?"

"The day Mr. Ross taught us the first motto?" David asked.

"No, David, the day before that—the day we saw that movie about the Nazi concentration camps. The day I was so upset. Remember? No one could understand how all the other Germans could have ignored what the Nazis were doing and pretended they didn't know."

"Yeah?" David said.

Laurie looked up at him. "David, do you remember what you said to me at lunch that afternoon?"

David tried to recall for a moment, but then shook his head.

"You told me it could never happen again."

David looked at her for a second. He felt himself smiling **ironically**. "You know something?" he said. "Even with

....

utterly completely
ironically even though he was not happy

the meeting with that national leader at the rally this afternoon—even though I was part of it, I still can't believe it's happening. It's so insane."

"I was just thinking the same thing," Laurie said. Then **an idea struck her**. "David, let's go back to school."

"Why?"

"I want to see him," she said. "I want to see this leader. I swear, I won't believe this is really happening until I see it for myself."

"But Mr. Ross said it was for Wave members only."

"What do you care?" Laurie asked him.

David shrugged. "I don't know, Laurie. I don't know if I want to go back. I feel like . . . like The Wave got me once and if I go back it might get me again."

"No way," Laurie laughed.

....

an idea struck her she got an idea

CHAPTER 17

It was incredible, Ben Ross thought as he walked toward the auditorium. Ahead of him, two of his students sat at a small table in front of the auditorium doors, checking membership cards. Wave members were streaming into the auditorium, many carrying Wave banners and signs. Ross couldn't help thinking that before **the advent of The Wave**, it would have taken a week to organize so many students. Today it had taken only a few hours. He sighed. So much for the **positive side of** discipline, community, and action. He wondered, if he was successful in **"deprogramming" the students from** The Wave, how long it would be before he'd begin seeing sloppy homework again. He smiled. Is this the price we pay for freedom?

....

the advent of The Wave The Wave was created

positive side of good things about

"deprogramming" the students from changing how the students thought about

As Ben watched, Robert, wearing a jacket and tie, came out of the auditorium and exchanged salutes with Brad and Brian.

"The auditorium is full," Robert told them. "Are the guards in place?"

"They are," Brad said.

Robert looked pleased. "Okay, let's check all the doors. Make sure they're all locked."

Ben rubbed his hands together nervously. It was time to go in. He walked toward the stage entrance and noticed that Christy was there waiting for him.

"Hi." She kissed him quickly on the cheek. "I thought I'd wish you luck."

"Thanks, I'll need it," Ben said.

Christy straightened his tie. "Did anyone ever tell you you look great in suits?" she asked.

"Matter of fact, Owens said that the other day." Ben sighed. "If I have to start looking for a new job, I might be wearing them a lot."

"Don't worry. You'll do fine," Christy told him.

Ben managed a slight smile. "I wish I **had your faith in me**," he said.

....

had your faith in me believed that I can be successful, too

Christy laughed and turned him toward the stage door.
"Go get 'em, tiger."

The next thing Ben knew, he was standing near the side of the stage, looking out at the crowded auditorium filled with Wave members. A moment later Robert joined him there.

"Mr. Ross," he said, saluting, "all the doors are secure and the guards are in place."

"Thank you, Robert," Ben said.

It was time to begin. As he strode to the center of the auditorium stage, Ben glanced quickly toward the curtains behind him and then up at the projectionist's booth at the back of the room. As he stopped and stood between two large television monitors that had been ordered from the AV department that day, the crowd **burst spontaneously into** The Wave mottos, standing at their seats and giving The Wave salute.

"Strength Through Discipline!"

"Strength Through Community!"

"Strength Through Action!"

Before them, Ben stood motionless. When they had finished their chants, he held up his arms for silence. In

....

"Go get 'em, tiger." "Good luck."
burst spontaneously into suddenly began saying

an instant the huge roomful of students went silent. Such obedience, Ben thought sadly. He looked out over the large crowd, aware that this was probably the last time he would be able to hold their attention so firmly. Then he spoke.

"In a moment our national leader will address us." And turning he said, "Robert."

"Mr. Ross, yes."

"Turn on the television sets."

Robert turned on both sets and the **picture tubes** grew bright and blue, with as yet no image. Throughout the auditorium, hundreds of eager Wave members **hunched** forward in their seats, staring at the blank blue tubes and waiting.

Outside, David and Laurie tried a set of auditorium doors, but found them locked. They quickly tried a second set, but found those locked also. But there were more doors to try, and they ran around the side of the auditorium looking for them.

The television screens were still blank. No face appeared on the screen and no sounds came from the speakers.

....

picture tubes television screens
hunched leaned

Around the auditorium students began to **squirm and murmur** with anxiety. Why wasn't anything happening? Where was their leader? What were they supposed to do? As the tension in the room continued to build, the same question passed through their minds over and over: What were they supposed to do?

From the side of the stage, Ben looked down at them, as **the sea** of faces stared back at him anxiously. Was it really true that **the natural inclination of people was to look** for a leader? Someone to make decisions for them? Indeed, the faces looking up at him said it was. That was the awesome responsibility any leader had, knowing that a group like this would follow. Ben began to realize how much more serious this "little experiment" was than he'd ever imagined. It was frightening how easily they would put their faith in your hands, how easily they would let you decide for them. If people were destined to be led, Ben thought, this was something he must make sure they learned: to question thoroughly, never to put your faith in anyone's hands blindly. Otherwise . . .

From the center of the audience a single frustrated student suddenly jumped up from his seat and shouted at

....

squirm and murmur move around and talk quietly
the sea hundreds
the natural inclination of people was to look people would automatically look

Mr. Ross, "There is no leader, is there!"

Shocked students around the auditorium quickly turned as two Wave guards rushed the offender out of the auditorium. In the confusion that followed, Laurie and David were able to slip in through the door the guards had opened.

Before the students had time to think about what had just happened, Ben strode to the center of the auditorium stage again. "Yes, you have a leader!" he shouted. That was the **cue** Carl Block had been waiting for as he hid backstage. Now he pulled back the stage curtains to reveal a large movie screen. At the same moment, Alex Cooper, in the projection room, **flicked** on a projector.

"There!" Ben shouted at the auditorium full of students. "There is your leader!"

The auditorium was filled with gasps and exclamations of surprise as the gigantic image of Adolf Hitler appeared on the screen.

"That's it!" Laurie whispered excitedly to David. "That's the movie he showed us that day!"

"Now listen carefully!" Ben shouted at them. "There is no National Wave Youth Movement. There is no leader. But

....

cue signal
flicked turned

if there was, *he* would have been it. Do you see what you've become? Do you see where you were headed? How far would you have gone? Take a look at your future!"

The film left Adolf Hitler and focused on the faces of the young Nazis who fought for him during World War Two. Many of them were only teenagers, some even younger than the students in the audience.

"You thought you were so special!" Ross told them. "Better than everyone outside of this room. You traded your freedom for what you said was equality. But you turned your equality into superiority over non-Wave members. **You accepted the group's will over your own convictions**, no matter who you had to hurt to do it. Oh, some of you thought you were **just going along for the ride**, that you could walk away at any moment. But did you? Did any of you try it?

"Yes, you all would have made good Nazis," Ben told them. "You would have put on the uniforms, turned your heads, and allowed your friends and neighbors to be persecuted and destroyed. You say it could never happen again, but look how close you came. Threatening those who wouldn't join you, preventing non-Wave members from

....

You accepted the group's will over your own convictions
You allowed what the group wanted to be more important than what you felt was right and wrong

just going along for the ride not really a part of it

sitting with you at football games. Fascism isn't something those other people did, it is right here, in all of us. You ask how could the German people do nothing as millions of innocent human beings were murdered? How could they claim they weren't involved? What causes people to **deny their own histories**?"

Ben moved closer to the front of the stage and spoke in a lower voice: "If **history repeats itself**, you will all want to deny what happened to you in The Wave. But, if our experiment has been successful—and I think you can see that it has—you will have learned that we are all responsible for our own actions, and that you must always question what you do rather than blindly follow a leader, and that for the rest of your lives, you will never, ever allow a group's will to **usurp** your individual rights."

Ben paused for a moment. So far he'd made it sound like they were all at fault. But it was more than that. "Now listen to me, please," he said. "I owe you an apology. I know this has been painful to you. But in a way it could be argued that none of you are as at fault as I am for leading you to this. I meant The Wave to be a great lesson for you and perhaps I succeeded too well. I certainly became more of a leader than

....

deny their own histories pretend that nothing happened; pretend that the Holocaust did not happen

history repeats itself you act like the Germans acted

usurp replace; take away

I intended to be. And I hope you will believe me when I say that it has been a painful lesson for me too. All I can add is, I hope this is a lesson we'll all share for the rest of our lives. If we're smart, we won't dare forget it."

The effect on the students was staggering. All around the auditorium they were slowly rising from their seats. A few were in tears, others tried to avoid the eyes of those next to them. All looked stunned by the lesson they had learned. As they left they discarded their posters and banners. The floor quickly became littered with yellow membership cards and all thoughts of military posture were forgotten as they slunk out of the auditorium.

Laurie and David walked slowly down the aisle, passing the **somber** students **filing out of** the room. Amy was coming toward them, her head bowed. When she looked up and saw Laurie she burst into tears and ran to hug her friend.

Behind her, David saw Eric and Brian. Both looked shaken. They stopped when they saw David and for a few moments the three teammates stood in an awkward silence.

"**What a freak-out**," Eric said, his voice hardly more than a mumble.

David tried to shrug it off. He felt bad for his friends.

....

somber saddened
filing out of leaving
What a freak-out I cannot believe we acted just like the Nazis

"Well, it's over now," he told them. "Let's try and forget it . . . I mean, let's try not to forget it . . . but let's forget it at the same time."

Eric and Brian nodded. They understood what he meant even if he hadn't exactly made sense.

Brian made a **rueful** face. "I should've known it," he said. "The first time that Clarkstown linebacker broke through and **sacked** me for a fifteen-yard loss last Saturday. I should've known it was no good."

The three teammates shared a short chuckle and then Eric and Brian left the auditorium. David walked down toward the stage where Mr. Ross stood. His teacher looked very tired.

"I'm sorry I didn't trust you, Mr. Ross," David said.

"No, it was good that you didn't," Ross told him. "You showed good judgment. I should be apologizing to you, David. I should have told you what I was planning to do."

Laurie joined them. "Mr. Ross, what's going to happen now?" she asked.

Ben shrugged and shook his head. "I'm not sure I know, Laurie. We still have quite a bit of history to cover this semester. But maybe we'll take just one more period to

....

rueful sorry, regretful
sacked tackled

discuss what happened today."

"I think we should," David said.

"You know, Mr. Ross," Laurie said. "In a way I'm glad this happened. I mean, I'm sorry it **had to come to this**, but I'm glad it worked out, and I think everyone learned a lot."

Ben nodded. "Well, that's nice of you, Laurie. But I've already decided this is one lesson I'm going to skip in next year's course."

David and Laurie looked at each other and smiled. They said good-bye to Mr. Ross and turned to leave the auditorium.

Ben watched Laurie and David and the last of the former members of The Wave leave the auditorium. When they were gone and he thought he was alone, he sighed and said, "Thank God." He was relieved that it had ended well, and thankful that he still had his job at Gordon High. There would still be a few angry parents and **incensed faculty members to smooth over**, but in time he knew he could do it.

He turned and was about to leave the stage when he heard a sob and saw Robert leaning against one of the

....

had to come to this went this far and people got hurt

incensed faculty members to smooth over he would have to apologize to other angry teachers

television sets, **tears running down his face**.

Poor Robert, Ben thought. **The only one who really stood to lose in this whole thing.** He walked toward the trembling student and put his arm around his shoulder. "You know, Robert," he said, trying to cheer him up, "you look good in a tie and jacket. You ought to wear them more often."

Through his tears, Robert managed a smile. "Thanks, Mr. Ross."

"What do you say we go out for a bite to eat?" Ben said, leading him off the stage. "There are some things I think we should talk about."

....

tears running down his face crying

The only one who really stood to lose in this whole thing.
Robert would be affected the most by the end of The Wave since he would go back to being an outcast.

BEFORE YOU MOVE ON...

1. **Summarize** Describe what happens at the rally to announce The Wave's new leader.

2. **Mood** Reread pages 183–185. How does the mood of the rally change? What do the students realize?